It is towards the [...]
Tony, George and S[...]
she always run awa[...] approach and why
won't she ever speak? The boys follow her and discover
that she lives with the Toad Lady, a formidable woman
whom the boys suspect of being a witch. As the boys
watch the two concocting spells Tony breaks away and
discovers the situation is not as it seems . . .

Toby Forward is highly regarded as an accomplished
writer for children. His books are characterized by their
unpatronizing style. In *The Toad Lady* he has tackled
the issue of disability with sensitivity and real
understanding.

The TOAD LADY
Toby Forward
Illustrated by Pat Tayler

PUFFIN BOOKS

PUFFIN BOOKS

Published by the Penguin Group
Penguin Books Ltd, 27 Wrights Lane, London W8 5TZ, England
Penguin Books USA Inc., 375 Hudson Street, New York, New York 10014, USA
Penguin Books Australia Ltd, Ringwood, Victoria, Australia
Penguin Books Canada Ltd, 10 Alcorn Avenue, Toronto, Ontario, Canada M4V 3B2
Penguin Books (NZ) Ltd, 182–190 Wairau Road, Auckland 10, New Zealand

Penguin Books Ltd, Registered Offices: Harmondsworth, Middlesex, England

First published by Andersen Press Limited 1991
Published in Puffin Books 1993
1 3 5 7 9 10 8 6 4 2

Printed in England by Clays Ltd, St Ives plc

For Alice

1

Buried Alive

'Yes. Yes. It's falling.'

'Oh. Help!' shouted George.

'Watch out! It's coming down.'

The boys, three of them, lay on their backs, looking up to the square, stone tower of the old church above them as it twisted and lurched, threatening to bury them in a heavy tumble of brown stone. Their squeals of terror carried across the empty playground.

Clouds, fresh, white and clumpy, rolled easily through the clear blue sky. The tower of the church solidly stood. But if you squinted beyond it, keeping your eyes on the moving clouds, it reared and buckled, slid over and toppled.

'Crash,' yelled Tony.

'Dead. All dead,' groaned Steve.

'Shut up if you're dead.'

Steve punched George.

'You're dead.'

George scrambled round, flinging soft punches over Steve's face and chest. They rolled over and over, scuffling. Tony sat up, scratched his knees and looked at them.

Steve's back hit the raised wall of the graveyard and they stopped rolling. George, a year younger than Steve but quite a lot taller and heavier, wrenched him down and sat across his chest. Steve was caught tight but still wriggled and fought. George quietly boxed him around the sides of the head.

'Dead. All dead.'

'No,' Steve argued.

George kept up the soft blows.

'Dead, Steve. Come on. You're dead.'

Tony moved from the dusty ground and climbed the high graveyard wall. He ignored George and Steve and screwed up his eyes against the light to look at the powdery yellow fields of wheat falling away down the gentle slope. Behind him the old church, no longer moving against the few puffy clouds, but fixed and handsome, firm on its hilltop, blessing the surrounding countryside as it had done for over eight hundred years. Set into the tower was a clock that had an hour hand, but no minute hand.

'The people who put that clock in didn't need to know the minutes,' Mrs Hodgson had said. Mrs Hodgson was the headmistress of the little village school that Tony could see beside the church if he

twisted his head to the right.

'Why not?' someone always asked when she told a new class about the clock.

'Because,' Mrs Hodgson would explain, with pleasure, her chubby neck folding above the collar of her blouse, 'because they didn't have buses and trains to catch. They didn't have televisions and the wireless to listen to at the right time.'

The class gasped. No television. No radio.

'What about school?' Tony had asked.

'They came when the bell rang and went home when they were told.'

Mrs Hodgson smiled as she told them. She was very old. Perhaps she remembered it? Perhaps she had rung the bell when there were no televisions and no trains. She looked as though she was sad that it was not like that now. But the class leaned on one another, clutching their heads and pretending to cry. No television!

The smile dropped from Mrs Hodgson's face. She glared at them.

'Stop that!' she snapped. 'Get on, now, or you'll not be needing a minute hand either. You'll all be here after school until I say so.'

And they would. Mrs Hodgson never went home. Mrs Hodgson didn't need to go home. She just pushed open a door in the side of the classroom and she was in her living room. The old school was a single building with two classrooms and a little house. The infants were taught in one classroom by

Miss Wilson, who came every day on her bike from the next village, Barton Parva. Mrs Hodgson taught the juniors all together in the next room, and then there was her house.

When she kept them in after school, Mrs Hodgson would open the door to her living room and Miss Wilson would go in with her. There they sat, drinking tea together, until Mrs Hodgson thought they had been punished enough, then she would come through, stand in front of the class and lead them in the last prayer. Everything seemed to happen with a prayer in the school, even punishment.

Before dinner, Miss Wilson would bring the little ones in and she would sit at the piano while they all sang.

'Thank you for the world so sweet
Thank you for the food we eat
Thank you for the birds that sing
Thank you, God, for everything
Amen '

Tony could never understand how one second Mrs Hodgson could be all smiling and happy, and then the next, just because they were joining in and laughing too, she was snapping at them and threatening to keep them in.

He was wondering about it when the sound of laughter pinched him into looking over at George and Steve.

Steve wouldn't admit that he was dead and he

and George had given up the point and were rolling on the ground together, too lazy to pretend to fight any more.

'You're filthy,' Tony called over to them.

They stopped, stood up and looked at their clothes. Tony was right.

The summer holidays were nearly over. It had been long and hot and dry, and the ground along the side of the graveyard wall that lead to the school was baked hard. The pretend fight had rubbed their shirts and shorts along the path, until the boys were covered with fine brown dust.

They looked at each other, bothered for a moment, then each caught the eye of the other and his worried look, and this made them laugh aloud. They always laughed at everything when they were together. Mrs Hodgson would not let them sit anywhere near each other in class. Tony watched them, thought about the row they would get into when they got home, then shrugged his shoulders. It wasn't his problem.

Tony liked being with George and Steve, but they were always doing things without him. Not spitefully, not like when people say, 'You aren't coming with us'. They always went around together, all three of them. But George and Steve were together, even when he was there.

It was Tony who had thought of the game with the church falling down. Lying there one day, at playtime, he had glanced up, and the rushing clouds over the tower had for a moment really made him think that it was falling. He showed Steve and George how to do it, how to lie there and look and pretend that the tower was going to crush them under its broken weight. They had liked the idea, and sometimes they played it with him, like today; but they quickly got bored and started to punch and cuff each other, while Tony could lie for many minutes on his own thinking about the horrible weight of the brown stones tumbling on to him.

'What are we going to do?' asked George.

He and Steve had hitched themselves up the side of the wall and were sitting next to Tony, swinging their legs.

'Bury you,' shouted Steve, and he pushed George back and started grabbing handfuls of graveyard earth, dry and crumbly, and dropping it on to George.

There was another, shorter struggle, which George won again. They only fought until the giggles came, then stopped suddenly, like a television that has been turned off.

'Well?' George asked.

'I don't know,' said Tony.

Steve was trying to get the dirt from his clothes, but it clung wetly to them.

Sweat had made him damp and clammy.

'I'm hot.'

Tony looked at him.

'So you should be.'

'Let's go in the church.'

'No.'

'We can play ghosts.'

'I don't want to.' Tony knew that George and Steve would only shout and mess about in the church and he hated that.

'Come on then,' said Steve, and he swung his legs over the wall and marched up to the door of the church.

Tony stayed still. George grinned at him.

'Coming?'

'No.'

Tony hoped that if he stayed on the wall, George would stay too and Steve would have to come back. Steve couldn't play on his own. George wriggled.

'It could be fun,' he said.

'No. It's silly.'

'What?'

'Ghosts. There aren't ghosts. It's only a church.'

'It's only a game,' said George.

'It's silly.'

'What then?'

Tony thought hard, but didn't know what to say. There was the railway line. There was the brook and the ford. Or they could go over the fields to the haystack and climb over that. They had done all these things during the long holiday, but they could do them again. He wanted to suggest one, but was frightened that George would say no. He knew that George would do what Steve said.

'I don't know.'

'Well then,' said George. 'Might as well go into the church.'

He followed up the path. Near to the porch he turned.

'Come on. It's hot. Let's go in.'

Tony nodded. George disappeared.

It was very hot. The few clouds that had made it look as though the tower was falling had gone. The slight breeze had dropped and the August sun burned down, turning the boys' skin brown and ripening the tight clusters of seed that clung to the stems of wheat in the fields.

On the path, Tony passed the headstones marking the old graves of the people who had lived and died in his village hundreds of years ago. People who had not needed to know the minutes, and now didn't need to know the hours either. Tony thought of them cold and quiet below the ground while he walked in the fierce heat above them. Had they looked over this hillside at the slowly ripening wheat and smelled the thick, lovely air of August? Had they dragged feet through the dusty paths of the village, looking for tiny fish darting in the water at the ford, water that seemed cold enough to break even on the hottest day? Perhaps one of them had stretched out on his back beneath the tower and watched the clumps of summer clouds fly past?

Tony stopped and rubbed his hand over the warm, rough surface of a stone, eaten away by weather and overgrown with lichen, giving it a greenish, living texture, like a lizard's skin.

The path led through the graves, up to the church porch. Beyond, the door gaped open into cool darkness. George and Steve had left it open behind them. Tony's eyes, used to the bright sun, could not make out any shape or movement through the door. No sound drifted through, escaping into the summer air. It was as though, pushing through the heavy oak slab, they had walked into a past of darkness, a cold and ghostly silence. Tony imagined them, spiralling through time into the days when the clocks had only one hand. He saw them, buried alive in the echoing hollow of the church's belly.

With a small feeling of sickness in his stomach, he stepped nervously from the bright summer day into the eerie gloom.

'George,' he called, gently.

'Steve?'

There was no answer.

Tony hesitated, then moved forward.

2

In the Darkness

A small fair girl, with a pigtail watched the boys scuffling in the dirt. She saw them sit together on the wall. Then she watched as the smallest one, with the very dirty clothes, left the others to go into the church. Her interest grew as the other two swung their legs and talked, kicking the backs of their heels against the crumbly stone wall of the graveyard, ruining the leather on their shoes. When the biggest boy, the one with the tight curly brown hair, followed the smaller boy, she pressed herself against the tree she was hiding behind.

Now that the third boy was alone, it seemed possible that he might look around him, might see her. She thought it would be pleasant to talk to him, but was nervous at the thought. Talking was so difficult, especially to strangers.

At last, the third boy stood up, dusted the back of his shorts with his hands, and followed his friends. Were they friends, she wondered. They seemed to spend a lot of time fighting. But, perhaps that was what they liked. She had been frightened when they started to punch but no blood came, and no bruises, and they laughed all the time, as though they were being tickled. She couldn't hear their voices, of course, so she was not sure whether they were shouting in anger or joy.

She was about to follow the third boy towards the church, when he stopped. Had he heard her? She froze, hoping that he would not turn. But he only reached out his hand and stroked it against a gravestone, like stroking a dog.

It disturbed her to see him looking down at the grave and caressing the headstone. Despite the great heat she shivered a little. She was dressed for summer in a light cotton dress, rather faded, and almost a size too small. She had worn it last year too. Then it had been just too big. Her mother had said she would grow into it, and she had, but it fitted her perfectly in the middle of the winter when it was too cold to wear it so she had had two summers in it when it didn't quite fit.

She kept close to the rough trunk of a horse-chestnut tree, watching the boy at the graveside. The bark, pitted and gouged, pressed small, irregular patterns into her skin, through the dress. Above her, buried in the spread of broad green leaves, were the spiky knobs of the conkers. Still green and juicy, the sun would soon heat the moisture from them, ripening and tanning them into hard, brown, shiny fruit with their dry husks dropping away. Then they would be ready to pierce with broad needles, and string through, and knot for the boys to smash together in competition.

But now, she watched this boy finish the walk up the path and pause at the church door. Tony had no idea he was being watched as he hesitated at the dark opening.

'Come on, George,' he called. 'I know you're there.'

Only silence answered him.

'Steve.'

Nothing.

He stepped into the pool of gloom.

'Great, fat wobbly bellies,' he shouted, hoping to make Steve laugh.

The stillness was complete.

Tony pressed the back of his hand against his mouth and blew over it, making a loud, wet rude noise with his tongue. Steve would have to laugh if he heard that in church.

There was no movement, no sound.

Tony walked out again, glad to feel the sun on his shirt and his bare arms, hear the comforting crying of the birds and see the wheat move lazily as a breeze brushed it. He screwed his eyes up against the sudden brightness, before he could get used to the glare. The girl dodged away from view. She dropped to the ground behind the broad, flat stone that Tony had stroked and wondered at.

Tony looked again through the door, ashamed at his nervousness. He knew they were hiding in there and that they would laugh at him if he didn't go in and find them, but he still wondered if something horrible had happened to them? Perhaps someone had been hiding in there and had hurt them as they had gone in one at a time. He would be waiting now, waiting for his third boy. He had heard Tony. He knew he was there. Silly, childish memories of Hansel and Gretel climbed into his mind and sat there, teasing him. A witch was waiting there to lock him in her cage and fatten him up. Already she had snapped off George's fingers and popped them in her mouth, a snack between meals.

This was too silly. There were no witches. Old tramps didn't lurk around in ordinary village churches waiting to attack boys one at a time. People didn't get sucked through time tunnels into the past to meet the people buried in the graves around the church. George and Steve were playing a trick on him, and he would go in and look for them.

The girl raised her eyes above the curved top of the headstone as Tony went back into the blackness. This time he strode straight in, hoping to dismay the others with his confidence.

In the winter, the walls of the church stored up cold and damp. Now the sun, after weeks of blazing down, was forcing the wetness from the brown prison stones, making the church sticky and musty after the dry air outside.

Tony clattered through the church. He kicked the sides of the old oak pews. He slapped his hands against the thick, smooth, rounded pillars, wider than the old horse-chestnut tree trunk that the girl had hidden against.

Around him, in the windows, people stared down. Saints and prophets in multi-coloured glass sprang to life in the bright sun. He waved up to them, as old familiars.

'Morning Jeremy,' he shouted to Jeremiah.

'How d'you do, David?' he asked the old King of Israel with the flowing robes and splendid white beard, nothing like the boy who had gone out with his sling and stones to kill Goliath. Is that really what had happened to the boy, Tony used to wonder.

'Excuse me, Mary,' he asked God's mother who was smiling at him in her blue dress, 'but have you seen a couple of stupid boys pretending not to be here?'

Mary looked understandingly down but, of course, made no answer.

Tony stopped in front of the altar. He bowed because they had been taught always to do that. Then he turned and surveyed the church.

'Just the place to hide stupid toads,' he decided aloud. 'Now where would I hide if I was a toad?'

Still making a lot of noise, he peered into

corners, rattled cupboard doors, and stomped around. He found nothing. Slowly, his noise gave way and he was quiet, wondering.

He sat in a pew, near the front, and watched, and waited.

The quietness thickened around him and he shuddered.

At last, there was a scratching noise. Then a groan.

'Oaahh.'

Tony stayed still.

'OOOaaahhhhh.'

He slid along his pew to the end and hid by the thick pillar.

Thud. Thud. Thud. Hollow bumps from the floor.

'Ooooooooaaaaaaahhhhhh.'

Tony felt the top of his head tingle, but he still didn't move. He kept silent.

Thud. Thud. A hollow beating of a wooden drum. He imagined a dead hand rapping against a coffin lid somewhere deep beneath him in the vaults.

Still he said nothing, made no movement.

A muffled, deadly voice echoed through the Church.

'Has he gone?'

'Must have,' came a ghostly reply.

'Sure?'

'Think so.'

There was a banging and a thumping.

'Coward.'

The voice this time was more clear and it belonged to Steve.

From his dark shade by the pillar, Tony watched a head appear from behind the altar. It was followed by another, and then two boys stood up. Steve and George had found a way into the back of the wooden altar and hidden there. Their voices had been changed by the echoes into the booming, ghostly voices Tony had heard.

'He's run away,' said Steve.

They stepped from the altar. Tony waited for them to make their way to the door. They passed him, not looking for anyone, and as they drew away he sprang to his feet, yelling.

'Whhhooooooaaaahhh.'

George and Steve jumped and swung around, shouts of fear in their throats.

Tony dropped back to his pew. He roared with laughter.

'You fool,' Steve shouted, furious.

Tony had tears in his eyes from laughing so much.

'You should have seen your faces,' he gasped. 'Oh, dear.'

'Oh, shut up. Shut up.' Steve didn't know what else to say.

'Oh, dear. Oh dear. Your faces.'

'You coward.'

'Me? Me a coward. I didn't run away, but you were terrified.'

Steve turned to George.

'Come on,' he said. 'Let's get out. He's stupid.'

Tony looked at George, his laughter stopped.

'Well?' said Steve. 'Are you coming?'

George started to smile.

'Only a joke,' he said. 'And he frightened me.'

'Don't be stupid. We weren't frightened.'

'I was. So were you.'

'No.' Steve clenched his fists. 'No I wasn't.'

'Well, we were trying to frighten him, but he beat us,' said George.

'Come on, shake,' Tony offered, reaching out his hand. It was what they always did when things got difficult.

Steve looked at the hand.

'No,' he said. 'Forget it.'

And he left the church.

'Aren't you going with him?' Tony asked.

George thought for a moment.

'No. I don't think so.'

As he rushed out of the church, Steve banged into the girl from the horse-chestnut tree and the gravestone. She tumbled over, but he ignored her and ran down the path, through the high gate and off.

George and Tony heard the noise of her cry as she fell and went to see what was happening.

'Hello,' said Tony. 'What's going on?'

The girl was hurrying back to her feet and

turning to run down the path. She had not seen the boys and ignored the question. But George caught her arm and swung her around so that she looked directly at his face.

'Come on. Are you all right?' he asked.

'Yes. I'm fine.' The girl's voice was strange. It was low, like a man's, and some of the sounds were slurred as though she were drunk.

'He didn't mean . . .' began George, but the girl turned quickly and ran down the path away from them.

'Hi. Stop.' Tony called after her. 'Who are you?'

The girl disappeared behind the horse-chestnut trees and was gone.

'What do you think?' asked Tony.

George shrugged.

'She doesn't live round here,' he answered. 'Unless she's just moved in.'

'We'll see when school starts.'

Tony groaned.

'Not school. Don't think about it yet. There's two weeks of the holiday left.'

'All right, then,' agreed George. 'Maybe we'll see her around.'

Ready for their tea, they walked slowly towards the small group of council houses on the edge of the village. From his hiding place, Steve watched them stroll off, happy together, and he softly said the worst word he knew, over and over and over.

3

Fletcher's Brook

The two bikes raced down the hill, fighting for first place. George was a more powerful rider, but Tony's bike was better and he got to the water first.

To the south side of Barton Magna, Tony and George's village, ran a brook which wound its way past the council houses, disappeared through a tight copse, crossed the lane at a ford and finally emerged at Barton Parva, two miles away. In the boys' village it was known as Fletcher's Brook, or just 'Fletcher's'. By the time it had reached Barton Parva it was simply 'the Stream,' Fletcher being unknown there.

The villages themselves had also dropped part of their names, the locals calling them just 'Magna' and 'Parva'. It seemed that Barton and Fletcher, though famous in their time, had been forgotten now, fallen away, out of people's memories and story, leaving only their names uncertainly behind.

Tony's bike struck the water first and a muddy

spray fountained out behind it, soaking George.

'Creep. You creep,' he yelled.

Tony laughed and laughed, even though the water had also gone sideways, drenching the insides of his legs.

'Got you, got you,' he called over his shoulder.

But the ride up the other side of the ford was steep and George's extra strength made up for the difference in the bikes and he soon drew level with Tony. Putting out a strong hand, he pushed Tony's narrow ribs and sent him reeling off his bike and into the grassy bank.

'You slug,' Tony screamed, landing in a clump of stinging nettles.

George dropped from his bike, flinging it from him and pounced on Tony, shaking him.

'Say that again. Go on. Say it again.'

'You slug. Slug.' Tony winced in pain. 'Toad-eater. Slug.'

The nettles were whipping Tony's legs, but he didn't dare yell out in pain. George didn't seem even to notice, although he too was rolling in them.

George straddled Tony's chest and boxed his ears.

'Made me wet, did you? Called me names, did you?'

Then he fell off, choking with laughter, and slid down to the hot, tarmacked surface of the lane where his bike lay, scratched from a hundred rough and tumbles, the wheels spinning and whirring in the sunlight, gears clicking uselessly.

Tony slid down after and squatted next to him, trying to laugh too.

Did Steve and George really enjoy this? Did they like being bruised and stung, shaken and cuffed? How could they? Tony wondered at it, helplessly.

Since Steve had gone off the week before in the church, he had refused to speak to them. Repeated calls at his door had been no use. He was always out, alone. There was no one else in the village to play with. All the other boys in the school were bussed in during the term, so he only had George and Tony or himself, and now he didn't want them.

They looked for him at the railway line where they put coins on the hot, steel track for the engine wheels to flatten. They looked at the haystack where they built castles and forts. They looked in the churchyard.

He was nowhere. The involved pattern of fields and woods around the village was so complicated that there were too many places for him to disappear to away from their usual favourites. The ford was the place that Steve always liked best, so they were riding their bikes up and down the hill, through the small trail of muddy water that the summer had left there. Soon, if there was no rain, it would dry up completely.

Tony, stung and bruised from George's attentions to him, missed Steve a lot. George lay, half on the bank, half on the lane, panting with pleasure and still laughing. Although Tony and Steve were eleven and George was only ten, George was like an elder brother to them. He was two inches taller and he weighed more. His feet looked as though they didn't belong, as though his mother had bought them a size too big so that he could grow into them. One day he would, and then he would be huge.

'I don't know where he gets it from,' she said to her friends. 'His dad and me aren't big, are we? And the food he eats.'

George could certainly eat a lot. On days when the van brought stew to school to be served up for dinner in the juniors' classroom, the others couldn't touch it for the sticky smell of it that hung in the air for the last half hour of lessons, before it was served, while it waited in the hotplate in the school kitchen. That didn't bother George. Bolting his portion down in no time, he would quickly swap his plate, first with Tony, then with Steve, and eat theirs as well. Once, Mrs Hodgson had caught him, and shouted at him. Then she watched Tony while he ate his. Every mouthful made his stomach heave but she wouldn't let him stop. The food rolled around in his mouth, looking for a way through to his throat, growing smaller on his fork and bigger in his mouth.

He finished his portion, then stood up quickly, rushed out of the room and across the playground to the toilets. Half-way there, he threw up everything he had just forced down all over the play-ground.

Mrs Hodgson, who had followed him, watched, and when he had finished, led him to the cloakroom, gave him a mop and bucket and told him to clear it up.

'Cheats never thrive,' she said. 'Food is precious. If you had eaten your stew properly the first time this would never have happened.'

'You should tell your mum,' Steve advised him. But he didn't. No one told their mum anything like that, it wasn't worth it.

So George grew and grew, his clothes never lasting him a proper winter or summer like other people's.

'Try again?' he asked Tony, pointing to the ford.

'No.'

'Come on.'

'No. I wish Steve was here.'

George looked surprised.

'Why?'

'He likes the ford,' Tony replied.

'He could be here if he wanted.'

It was very simple for George. Steve was welcome, but he didn't want to come. So he could play on his own.

'I thought you liked Steve,' Tony asked.

'I do.'

'So, don't you want him?'

George thought.

'You're here,' he decided. 'I'm playing with you.'

Tony knew from his scratches and stings that this was true and wished even more that Steve would come back.

'Come on,' he said, getting up. 'Let's go somewhere.'

George followed willingly.

'Where?'

'Along the side of Fletcher's,' Steve pointed, 'and down towards Parva.'

George grinned and pushed his bike along with Tony.

The path at the side of the brook was bumpy and uneven, so they ditched their bikes in the bushes and made their way without them. George took off his shoes and socks and walked along the middle of the brook.

'Come on,' he invited Tony, but Tony looked at the muddy toes that George dragged squelchily out of the water at every step and shook his head.

The long, hot summer had dried out most of the council house gardens. Hoses were made illegal, and lawns and flower beds scorched brown in the sun. But here, alongside the brook where the countryside dipped down, making a bowl for the water to settle in, the trees and undergrowth remained green and fresh. Walking beneath the branches, on either side of the little channel, linked

31

overhead, and throwing a pale, green light on the boys, was strangely like walking through the church. The trunks of the trees like the sturdy pillars, their overhead branches the vaulting. Even bird noises were muted, and the boys lowered their voices, not in prayer, but in respect for the quietness they waded through.

They were not talking at all when they saw Steve.

George's face crinkled into a smile; he raised his arm, ready to shout over to Steve, when Tony grabbed his wrist and pulled it down. He placed his finger to his lips and made a shush signal. George closed his half-open mouth.

Steve was crouched low, his back to them, looking over a wall. Sometimes, without warning, he dipped his head below the level of the stones, waited, then raised it cautiously again. George and Tony watched him.

Tony pulled George from the water, his feet sticky with rich brown mud, and the two boys dropped down on to the brookside.

'Let's be careful,' he suggested.

'Creep up, and leap out and scare him,' said George.

'No.' Tony was fierce.

George looked at Tony for a suggestion.

'He's not talking to us because I did that in the church.' George nodded.

'If we frighten him now, he'll never talk to us again. All right?'

George agreed.

'What shall we do, then?' he asked. 'Go away?'

Tony shook his head.

'We want to play with him again, don't we?'

'I suppose so,' George agreed.

Tony looked at his knees, scuffed and grazed; his legs, bumpy with nettle stings; his clothes, smeared with dust and grime. Tony very much wanted Steve back for George to play with.

'Right, then. We've got to be careful.'

Tony suggested that he should make his way through the trees, away from the brook, and out into the open. Then he could walk fairly noisily towards Steve so that he could hear him. That would stop him being surprised.

'You stay here,' he said, 'looking at the water. I'll get Steve to come with me and creep up on you. We can jump out and frighten you, and then it'll be all right.'

George agreed. He settled himself down to wait, with his feet trailing in the slow water, trying to wash off the mud.

It was easy for Tony to clear a way through the trees, then sprint away quietly, so that he walked towards Steve in open view, whistling. As he drew near, Steve swung round, saw him and waved frantically. It was not a greeting, but a warning. Tony stopped. Steve waved his hands, palms downwards. Tony dropped to the ground and crept up to Steve.

'What is it?' he whispered.

'It's the girl. The one from the church.'

'What?' asked Tony.

Steve told him what was going on, and Tony whistled softly to show his dismay.

'Let's tell George,' he suggested. 'He's by Fletcher's.'

Steve looked doubtful.

'It's all right,' said Tony. 'We've missed you. Come on.'

George wasn't there when they reached the brook. Steve and Tony scouted around but there was no sign. They met up again where George had been sitting.

'Perhaps something's happened to him,' suggested Tony.

Just then, there was a horrid shriek, and a body fell down on to Steve's back, rolling him over. Tony yelled and sprang away. George had scrambled up the tree as soon as Tony had left and was waiting for them.

Steve punched at him, not playfully like he used to, but hard. George was astonished, and was about to punch back when Tony stepped in.

'Stop it. They'll hear us,' he hissed.

Steve and George froze.

'What?' asked George. Tony pointed to Steve.

'Tell him,' he said.

And Steve told George about the girl from the graveyard.

'She's gone into that house over there, over the wall. And she's on her own. Except,' and he paused here, 'except that that's where the Toad Lady lives. And she's in there with her.'

George shivered.

4

Frogspawn

The Toad Lady was a mystery. She came into the village from time to time, bought some things from Mrs Dean at the little shop or caught the bus into town.

'Are you sure it's her,' asked George.

'Course,' said Steve. 'You couldn't miss her, could you? Not like she looks like.'

George and Tony agreed.

In the spring, Fletcher's jumped and sang its way through the deep cut in the valley bottom. Melted winter snow and warmer March rain drained through the hillside and into the channel. The brook rose, climbing up the markers on the black-and-white pole at the side of the ford: one foot, two feet, three feet. The boys used to laugh. A brook with feet was funny enough, but the pole said that it could have as many as five; one more than a cow, one less than a wasp. The pole was old and had been put there before metres and centimetres appeared in the village school.

When the brook was really swollen, cars couldn't go through the ford and they had to drive an extra eight miles to go the long route to town through Barton Parva, Berksford and Hampton-in-Vale. Once, a stranger had tried to drive through when the water was licking the two foot-six mark on the pole. The car had sprayed water out at the sides on the way down, but the force of the current had dragged it back when it tried to mount the hill the other side. The engine stopped, water-logged; the electrics fused, and it came to rest in the middle, with the current still trying to feed it down stream to Parva. The driver sat for five minutes, with the water trickling through the gaps in the door-frames, then gave up. He climbed out of the window, waded to the road and fetched Mr Maple from his farm to tow it out with his tractor. Fletcher's looked peaceful enough now, but it could be dangerous.

In the spring the mist lurked in the bushes like a murderer waiting for a victim. Cold air rushed up the line of the brook and brought with it a slow, mournful howling as it swooped through the tall, naked trees. An old story in the village, older than anyone still alive, said that one spring a series of bodies had floated down the brook, one after another, their dead faces turned upwards, pale and bloated in the water. There were no marks on the bodies to show how they died. Their lungs were empty, so they had not drowned. For nine days they floated past, a new body every day, and then, they stopped. No one was reported missing, no one ever knew where they came from. They were supposed to be buried in an unmarked spot in the graveyard, in a common grave.

In the spring, when the mist still lurked in the bushes lining the banks of Fletcher's and the chill air brushed their faces, the boys had waded into the water in their wellingtons, collecting frogspawn to take home in jars. It clung to the weeds, looking sticky, but when you scooped your hands underneath it, it was icy cold in the sharp water, and the little black specks of eggs in their protective and nourishing jelly were slippery and smooth. If you got it early, the black specks were like full-stops in a book but later on, as the spring advanced, the spots grew cloudy and fatter; then you could stare into them and see pictures like looking into the fire, or watching the clouds swirl and change. The spots throbbed silently, not full stops any more, but little sentences about to be written.

George and Steve liked it best when the tadpoles burst out and then grew legs and turned into tiny green frogs. But Tony was disappointed with that. For him the first signs of life and movement promised variety and newness, as though each one could become something quite different; this one a crab, that one a bettle, this one a midget shark, that one a perfect, tiny elephant; and others, strange and different, no animals you'd had ever seen or dreamed about, not even in books with pictures of mermaids and monsters. All those dozens of identical frogs were far less exciting than the possibilities.

But the frogspawn was fun, no matter what it turned into, and every spring the boys were at Fletcher's scooping it up.

'Look at this one,' George had shouted, holding up a long line of spawn like a streamer. It writhed in his hands as though it was alive, a snake or a giant centipede, but that was just because it was so slippery that George was struggling to stop it slipping through his fingers back into the water.

'It's an arm,' he screamed. 'The arm of a corpse.'

Steve giggled. Tony looked around. They often joked about the bodies, but this was a cold, grey day, a day when murders might happen.

Steve growled, 'They're coming back. The bodies are coming back.'

'And so's the murderer, this time,' added George in a husky whisper. 'And he'll . . .'

'Put that down, you stupid child!'

The voice rang out through the trees arching over the brook.

George froze in alarm, and Steve and Tony swung their heads around, mouths open.

'This minute!' the voice boomed.

George let the band of spawn slither through his fingers and slop into the water, like a rat slipping into a hole.

'And come here.'

Tony gaped at the figure on the bank. It couldn't be true. It couldn't.

'Do you hear me?' it rapped.

'Don't go,' said Steve, looking as pale as Tony, but setting his face in a defiant grimace.

'Now!' it called.

George waded through the water and made his way to the owner of the voice.

It was the first time the boys had seen the Toad Lady, and her looks were as frightening as her loud, deep voice.

She was not tall, but then neither were they at that age, so she looked down on them. She was dressed like a man, thick corduroy trousers, heavy woollen jumper and a waxed jacket with a corduroy collar. Her legs were hidden in green wellingtons.

'You ridiculous creature,' she accused George.

He began to come to his senses after his fright.

'Look here,' he began.

'Look here! You have the cheek to tell me to look here!' she rumbled at him. 'Hi, you two,' she waved at Tony and Steve who were trying to look as though they weren't there, 'you come over here too.'

And over they came, slowly pushing their black wellingtons through the mud.

'Now then,' she said, looking at the three of them. 'What are you up to?'

'Collecting frogspawn,' Tony offered, holding up his jar to show her the eggs in their jelly.

She looked at it.

'You are,' she agreed. Her face was part-hidden under a tweed hat that swept down low, masking her. 'But he isn't,' she pointed to George.

'I am,' he argued.

'Silence.'

And they were quiet. Even Mrs Hodgson didn't talk to them like this. She threatened them with a punishment, or made nasty spiteful little comments that made the others laugh at them and brought the red to their faces, but the Toad Lady just told them what to do and they did it. There was something in her face that frightened them but they weren't sure what it was.

'Now then. This,' she pointed again at Tony's jar, 'is frogspawn. You can do what you like with it for all I care. You can eat it, paint it, put it in your wellingtons; you can pile it up, blow it up, or puke it up; I don't even care if you dredge every bit of it out of the brook and put it in your mother's bath for her to wallow in like a pig in muck.'

The boys stared up at her, unable to believe that a grown-up would speak like this.

'My mother's not a pig,' George began to say, but she interrupted him.

'Of course not. She's a perfectly decent woman, though you wouldn't think it to look at you.'

George snapped his mouth shut, frightened to offer any further argument.

'But I'm not interested in your mother,' she went on. 'The point is, you can do anything you want with the frogspawn, it doesn't matter. But that, young man, that you were waving around your head like a football scarf, that is not frogspawn. That is toadspawn, and that's something else entirely.'

'It's all the same,' said Steve.

'There you are,' she wagged her finger at him. 'I knew it.' Then she began.

'There are enough frogs around here to start a plague in Egypt. Decent enough little things, no harm in them, and they even do a bit of good, keeping a few flies down. I don't mind a frog.'

She said it the way the boys' mothers said 'I don't mind a chocolate', and they had thoughts of this wild woman dragging her hand through the muddy bottom of Fletcher's, bringing up a bright green wriggling frog, (legs waving and long tongue flicking) and popping it into her mouth. Her teeth snapped through the brittle bones, and the soft flesh, like the centre of a chocolate, spilled into her mouth.

'We don't eat them,' George said quickly.

'Of course you don't. Not even a boy like you,' she agreed.

'You said we did,' he added.

'No I didn't, did I?' she looked at the others, who nodded. This was very frightening.

'You said, take them home and eat them,' said Tony.

'Oh, I see. That's it, is it?'

They nodded.

'Well, I didn't mean you should. I meant it wouldn't matter if you did. There are so many of them.'

The boys were not at all convinced by this.

'Do you?' asked Steve.

'Me?'

'Yes. Do you eat them?'

The Toad Lady looked at them carefully. It was a problem, not being able to see her face properly, because you couldn't guess very easily what she was thinking. There was quite a long silence while she thought and they tried to look at her without her looking too closely at them.

At last she spoke.

'I might,' she said. 'I just might eat a frog every now and then.'

The boys dreadfully wanted to get away from her, but were frightened to go until she dismissed them. They didn't like the idea of turning their backs on her.

'Never mind the frogs, though,' she went on,

'it's this boy here I'm interested in.' She pointed at George again.

'You leave him alone,' Tony said.

'I'll leave him alone, if he'll leave that stuff alone.'

'That frogspawn?'

'How many times do I have to tell you, that's not frogspawn. It's toadspawn. It's very important.'

'Why?' asked Tony.

'At last. At last a sensible question. I thought none of you had it in you to ask one.'

They looked resentfully at each other; this was more like Mrs Hodgson, more like the grown-ups they knew.

'Toads aren't anything like as plentiful as frogs around here. In fact, they're quite rare. Have you ever seen one?'

The boys shrugged.

'Don't know?' she asked.

'No.'

'I thought not. You wouldn't know, would you. Well toads are a good bit bigger than frogs, at least as far as frogs and toads around here are concerned; it's not like that everywhere. And our frogs are green, but the toads are dark brown, just a bit greenish here and there. Now then, have you seen any toads?'

The boys looked at each other again.

'No.'

'There you are then. That's because they're

45

getting rare. They're lumpier than the frogs as well, with a warty skin.'

She didn't make them sound very nice at all, but she seemed to be very keen on them.

'And so,' she grew fierce again (her voice had been fairly pleasant and normal while she was describing the toads) 'when some poor toad manages to lay its eggs, not in a clumsy lump like your common frog, but delicately in a fine string like a rope of pearls, she doesn't want some gormless nitwit dragging them out of the water and swinging them round his head, does she?'

She stared at George while she asked this question, as though he had personally attacked every toad in the village.

'Does she?' she repeated. It was clearly not one of those questions that grown-ups ask where they don't expect you to answer because you all know what the answer is.

'No,' he mumbled.

'Right. You see nature didn't make the toad look very lovely, so she did something else instead. Underneath the toad's skin there are glands that make poison. This stops other animals eating the toad, but it does nothing to stop little boys, who ought to know better, from destroying her babies before they even get a chance to be born.

So don't you think you ought to leave them alone?'

'Yes,' George whispered.

'And the rest of you?'

They nodded.

'That's good, then.'

And then, without another word, she turned around and left, as suddenly as her voice had torn through the spring sunshine.

'Blind, blast and brrrrr!' said Steve when she was out of hearing. Steve sometimes swore a lot more richly than this, but the Toad Lady had alarmed him so much that he wasn't sure that she wouldn't spring out again without warning.

George had only just got to the age where he didn't cry if people shouted at him, and he looked as if he might now.

Tony stamped his feet in his boots because his toes had got cold standing still.

'Who is she?' he asked.

The others didn't know.

'Did you look at her?'

'What about it?'

'Well her face was sort of lumpy, wasn't it? And she was all in browns and browny-greens.'

George shouted.

'Toad Lady. She's the Toad Lady.'

'What's that?' Steve asked.

George shrugged.

'She eats toads as well,' said Tony.

'It's made her look like a toad,' Steve added.

'Maybe,' said George slowly. 'Maybe she's half toad-half human.'

'And she said poison.'

'Yes. That's right. Perhaps she collects them for their poison.' Steve looked serious.

'She killed them,' decided Tony.

'What?' demanded George.

'You know. In the brook. Dead bodies. She poisoned them with her toads.'

'No,' scoffed George.

'Yes,' Steve yelled agreement. 'Then slid their bodies from the bank and let them float down.'

'It was years ago,' argued George, with less conviction in his voice than he really felt.

Steve shrugged. 'She's old,' he said. 'Really old.'

After that, they saw her from time to time in the village but she never spoke to them, and they didn't know where she lived.

Now, way along Fletcher's almost to Parva, through the trees and set into a little clearing, they had found her house and the new girl was in there with her.

'What are they doing?' George asked.

'That's just it,' said Steve. They're sitting opposite each other at a table, making a spell.'

'What?'

'They aren't saying a word, just moving their hands like this.' He made a motion like a magician.

'What for?' asked Tony.

'Getting ready to kill some more,' said George.

'Why,' demanded Tony. 'Who?'

'They want us,' said Steve. 'For knocking her over the other day. 'Come and look.'

5

Spies

The Church, with its graveyard and wall around it, was like the gold centre of an archery target. The next ring was a group of old houses that had been there for varying lengths of time, but the newest was two hundred years old. They were the real village: some were large and impressive, the old vicarage, Church Farm, Glebe House, the pub; others were small, labourers' cottages and a row of almshouses. These last were old as well, and until recently had not had indoor lavatories, nor even running water in their sinks. Now, instead of housing farm workers and servants for the big houses, many of them were weekend houses for the people from the towns.

The boys did not live in any of these old houses. At one edge of the village, down the lane half a mile from the old part, was a cluster of council houses, tucked behind a clump of trees like a shameful secret. Visitors to the weekend cottages were surprised when they took an evening walk and found them squatting furtively like lepers outside the pale.

'What a shame', they thought, and were glad that the council houses were invisible from the village's heart.

The boys lived here. Steve's dad rode his bike into town every morning to drive a bus, although only one bus a week came through the village these days. George's dad worked for Mr Maple up at Glebe Farm, just as his family had always done. They had always lived in one of the cottages until the council built these houses and Mr Maple's father had told George's grandfather that he would be more comfortable here. Tony hadn't got a dad, but his mum cleaned for Mrs Trent at Glebe House and helped out a lot with occasional jobs in the pub and at Maple's farm when things were busy.

The Toad Lady lived near the village, but the boys had never discovered where. They didn't have much to do with Parva, so they had never walked right along to where Fletcher's turned into the Stream. Now, Steve led them to the wall around her house.

Her house was like the ones around the church, old and big, but being in the woods it had a huge garden, surrounded by a high wall. The garden was mainly grass, not neatly mown, but longish and brown in the summer's furnace. The grass was studded with a surprising number of wild flowers. On very bright days, the coloured windows in the church sprayed patterns of gems on the stone slabs of the floor. Tony looked at the wild flowers, speckling the grass and was reminded of the windows so strongly that he nearly looked to see if were any set in the high stone wall. A goat browsed among apple and pear trees which were heavy with unripe fruit.

'She doesn't do much,' said George, whose father kept their tiny patch of garden looking as orderly as a patterned carpet, and as closely clipped.

'Doesn't need to,' said Steve. 'She's got the goat.'

George sniffed. He thought his dad could tidy it up if he had it.

'Where's the girl?' asked Tony.

Steve drew them round the corner of the wall, pressing his finger to his lips. They kept their heads down, backs bent double.

'There.'

Cautiously, the boys lifted their heads above the top of the wall. Behind a window, criss-crossed with lead into clear lozenges, sat the Toad Lady and the girl.

'What they up to?' asked George.

Facing each other at a table in the window, the two were weaving a spell with their hands. First, the Toad Lady would tap her fingers on to the opposite palm, spread her hands together, like she was washing, sometimes tap her head softly with her fingertips. The girl watched intently, then made her

own magical contribution to the spell. Once, the Toad Lady shook her head vigorously and grabbed the girl's hand. Then she directed her to repeat what she had done until she was satisfied. At no time did either of them say a word to the other, but their eyes were intently on what was being conjured with the hand movements.

'She's got it wrong,' said Steve, when the Toad Lady grabbed the girl's hand.

'What?' demanded George.

'She's teaching her how to make spells,' Steve explained. 'I've been watching them for about half an hour.'

'What for?'

'For us,' said Steve. 'Must be, because we pushed her over.'

'I don't see why,' said Tony.

'Must be,' Steve insisted. 'I've been watching them.'

'I still don't think that means it's got to be us,' Tony persisted.

'Look. You know the Toad Lady hates us. Remember that day at Fletcher's when she let George have it for picking up the frogspawn.'

'Toadspawn,' Tony corrected him.

'Same thing. Spawn. You heard her. You heard her say it was poisonous. Remember?'

Tony nodded. He had to; it was true.

'But that doesn't mean she's magicking us now.'

'Course it does,' George spoke up.

Tony looked at him. He was right up next to Steve, just like he always had been.

'Maybe,' he agreed.

'Right,' said George, grinning at Steve.

'Good,' Steve continued. 'So what shall we do?'

Tony looked from George to Steve and then back from Steve to George. The last few days hadn't happened. They had never fallen out, Steve had never run off from the church, George had never said it didn't matter whether Steve played with them or not. They were together again, and Tony was on his own, like he had wanted.

'I don't care,' he said. 'Do what you want.'

He dropped his head, bent his back, and loped off, away from the Toad Lady's house, up the brook and back to his bike. George and Steve watched him for a moment, then scrutinized the house again.

Tony wondered what the feeling inside him was. His stings and bruises told him to be glad that Steve was back and that he and George could rough-house together again and leave him alone, but something else felt betrayed. He wasn't frightened of anything, but the churning in his stomach and the faintly sick feeling in his throat made him feel as though he was. He didn't understand it.

Back at the side of the brook, his bicycle lay next to George's. He grabbed it and pedalled away angrily. He forced his feet down hard so that he hit the water on the road like a train, spraying it out like a curse and spattering his trousers. He rode as fast as he could until he reached the church, then he flung the bike down on the path and lay below the wall, eyes fixed on the tower, watching it skew and bend under the enchanted clouds.

He went to the church a lot in the next few days. He still played with Steve and George. They were careful to come and collect him in the morning but he didn't want to be with them all day. After a while he made excuses and left them to scuffle and fight together, their faces contorted with the laughter that seemed to overwhelm them when they were grabbing and shoving one another.

'What's up?' his mother asked when he scuffed into the house, far too early for his tea.

'Nothing.'

'I can find you some jobs,' she offered.

'Oh, Mum. It's the holiday.'

'Fine holiday you're having,' she grumbled. 'Hanging around the house all day.'

'I'm out a lot,' he protested.

'Too much,' she complained.

'Well, if I'm out too much I can't be hanging around the house all day, can I?' Grown-ups were so stupid.

'You know what I mean.'

Tony knew all to well what she meant, so he kept quiet. She meant that she did not like him being with Steve and George all the time, but neither did she want him under her feet all day. So what was the point?

'Really,' she offered. 'I could find you some jobs.'

'In the garden,' he mumbled.

'Yes. And what's wrong with that, I'd like to know? You're good in the garden. Or I could ask Mrs Trent if she wants a hand. She'd pay you.'

Tony kicked the leg of the table and fiddled with a teaspoon.

'Come on, Tony,' said his mother, not so harshly this time. She put her arm around his shoulders but he shrugged it off.

'Too hot,' he complained. 'And I hate gardening.'

'You could help me,' she offered. 'In the house. Mrs Trent might pay you for that. I need some help, moving the heavy stuff to clean. My back plays up, and my shoulder.' She rolled her shoulders and rubbed her back, as though her rheumatism pained her then and there.

'Can't,' said Tony, scraping his chair back and standing up suddenly. 'Got to go and see George and Steve.'

'Please, Tony,' she asked. 'Think about it. You know you could use some extra pocket money.'

'All right,' he agreed.

'You'll do it?' she asked. 'I'll ask Mrs Trent.'

'All right, I'll think about it I mean,' he said.

'Got to go.'

He could see the signs and he wanted to get out. Quickly. If he wasn't fast enough she would start talking about his dad, and he couldn't stand that.

'I wish I could take you away,' she called to him. 'Properly. For a proper holiday. It's so difficult. Since your dad died we've . . .'

'Bye,' Tony called over his shoulder. He ran the bike along the path, jumped on and pedalled away.

'Stay a bit,' she called. 'You could read a book. You like that.' She stood in the doorway and watched him disappear. She rubbed her back absently, hardly noticing that the pain had begun to creep back in there and in her shoulder.

Tony spent a lot of time in the church and around the graveyard. The sun, unending now in its intense heat, loosened his bowels and upset him; it muddled his mind, making him light-headed and dizzy. Down the sides of the brook under the canopy of trees, and in the echoing solidness of the church the air was cooler and the light more gentle, and he felt relaxed and comfortable.

Three days after he saw the Toad Lady teaching the girl her spells, Tony found her in the church. She was still wearing the same thin cotton dress that she had worn when Steve had sent her hurtling down on the gravel of the graveyard path. Her knees were scabbed over, and one elbow was caked with a brown graze where the blood had oozed. She was kneeling on the floor in a side aisle when Tony opened the door and saw her.

He had walked quite normally into the church, not trying to creep up or make no noise, but she ignored the slamming of the heavy oak door, pretending to be absorbed in what she was looking at.

Tony was unnerved. If she had turned her head he could have smiled at her, but she gazed stead-fastly at the floor in front of her. He moved away from the door, trying not to creep up on her, but embarrassed to clump along like a lout.

His bangings and bumps echoed around the building until they were soaked up by the old stones. He didn't know where to walk. He couldn't ignore her, and he didn't want to walk straight up to her. He had not come into church to do anything in particular, just to escape the great heat and to sit idly looking at the windows, the carved wood and chiselled stone.

At last, he made his way to the girl.

'Hello,' he said, looking over her shoulder from above.

Still she ignored him. It didn't seem right. He hadn't done anything to her.

'Look here,' he said. 'I didn't knock you over.' And he reached a hand out to touch her shoulder.

The effect was startling. He could have dashed the heavy blade of a sharp sword against her, bringing off her arm at the shoulder and she would not have been more alarmed. She scrambled forward along the stone slabs, like an injured puppy, jerking her head round to look at him.

'I'm sorry,' he said. 'Hey, look. I didn't mean to frighten you.'

She steadied herself, still on the floor, but now sitting inelegantly bunched up.

'Look. I'm sorry,' he said again.

The girl's face began to lose its desperate fear and recover.

'That's all right,' she said at last, in the funny voice that Tony now remembered.

'Here,' he held his hand out to help her up. She smiled shyly and took it, pulling herself to her feet.

'Look at your knees,' said Tony, pointing to the scabs.

The girl looked down, shrugged her shoulders.

'It doesn't matter,' she said. 'Look,' and she twisted her left arm so that Tony could see the thick graze on the elbow.

'He didn't mean to,' Tony explained. 'You were in his way and he didn't see you.'

'I don't mind.'

'Why did you run away?' he asked.

The girl hesitated before she answered, and something in her face told Tony that she wasn't telling the truth.

'He took me by surprise,' she lied.

'Oh.'

Tony didn't like her lying to him, but didn't feel

he could challenge her. It was funny how you knew, he thought. That must be what he looked like when he lied to Mrs Hodgson. No wonder she always knew.

'What about your friend?' she asked.

'What?'

'Why was he running away like that?'

Tony remembered how ashamed Steve was when he had frightened him, and he didn't want to tell her. It was Steve's secret, not his.

'Oh, nothing,' he lied. 'He was just in a hurry to get home.'

As he looked at the girl, he knew that she had seen his lie, too, so they were even.

'Look, never mind that. What are you doing?'

The girl pointed to the floor. Set into the stone slabs was the figure of a woman, worked in brass. It was very old, and the sharp outlines had been rubbed smooth by the feet that had walked over it. Usually there was a scrap of carpet covering it, but the girl had dragged this aside.

'Oh, her,' said Tony.

The girl looked disappointed.

'Don't you like her?'

'I don't know,' said Tony. 'I've never thought about it.'

The girl crouched down.

'Look,' she said . 'She's more than five hundred years old. See, 1479. That's when she died.'

'I never thought about it before, but now . . .'

began Tony.

The girl carried on talking in her strange, deep voice, as though he hadn't spoken.

'And she had a dog, look. Here he is, at her feet.'

Tony looked more closely than he ever had before, and saw that the woman had small pointy-toed shoes, and they were resting on a dog. Above the toes, she was lying flat on her back, her arms crossed over her chest, eyes open looking out at them.

'Just think,' the girl went on. 'Until someone covered her up with this rug, she lay here for five hundred years, staring up at the ceiling.' She paused a moment before she said the next thing, and she looked at him to see what he would do.

'Just like you do. Just like you, lying outside staring up at the sky.'

'How do you know about that?' he asked quickly, not liking to think that he had been spied on.

'I see you. That first day when he knocked me over, I was watching the three of you.'

'Yes,' he agreed.

'And on your own. You come here on your own and look at the sky.'

Tony felt foolish, and the blood painted his cheeks.

'It doesn't matter,' she said. 'I like it. It's good.'

Tony looked strangely at her. Perhaps Steve was right. Perhaps she did make spells with the Toad Lady. Why else should she spy on him? She smiled again, and that put him at his ease, until the next thing that she said, and that made him shiver with a fear that affected him like too much sun, gripping his tummy and making his head swim.

6

Staring Up

Tony remembered what Steve had said about the spells and about the Toad Lady catching toads to get the poison out of them so that she could use it on people. He looked at the girl and wondered what she had been doing with the Toad Lady that afternoon behind the leaded lozenges of the old windows.

She looked ordinary enough, with her thin arms and legs and the faded dress just too small for her, but she had been there in the Toad Lady's house behaving in a very odd way.

Beneath his knees, the stone slabs of the floor were very cold, and the girl was tracing her fingers lazily over the brass picture of the long-ago lady, feeling the cold of the bright metal. The heat outside didn't penetrate the thick walls. The cold of hundreds of winters was stored up in there, more powerful than the warm breezes that brushed the tower and the buttresses.

Even the noises were mute. Outside, the grass was vibrant with the buzz and whirr and click of scaly insect bodies; birds punctured the summer silence with sharp points of sound; over the fields modern machines cut through swathes of hay slicing the stems and bundling it up into feed for the winter; trains pushed along the bright metal track, thumping and screeching, dragging hot air behind them as the sound grew and faded, up and down; even Fletcher's, crawling its muddy path to Parva through the woods, past the Toad Lady's house inside its walled garden, made a selfish, gurgling noise; but in here, in the church, the noises were locked out. Tony felt the silence closing in on him, hunting him, cornering him in the old stones. He didn't like even to move his feet against the oak sides of the pews, fearing to shatter the quiet.

The girl's voice, thick and heavy, man-like and slurred, seemed part of the silence, not foreign to it.

'See her eyes,' she directed Tony.

He looked at them.

'They stare up and up.'

He nodded.

'Just think; every night when we're lying in our beds, she's here, looking up into the darkness. What does she see?'

Tony made himself think of her, and thought of his own body in her place, engraved on brass, lying cold and silent in the locked, empty church. It hurt him somewhere to imagine it.

66

'Night after night,' the girl went on. 'Just looking into the darkness; for hundreds of years.'

Tony looked at the brass figure. Her face was plump and wide, but there was no roundness to it, no life or laughter, just a flat, blank look, knowing and secret.

'She's just a picture,' he said, trying to break the strange spell the girl was casting. She paid no attention to him. He grabbed her arm and she looked up at his face.

'Do you hear me?' he asked. 'She's just a picture.'

'Oh, yes,' the girl agreed, 'just a picture.'

They both looked one last time, then the girl dragged the scrap of carpet over the figure.

'There now, now she can't see anything. Perhaps she hates us for doing that, making her blind.'

Tony moved away, glad to have covered the blank face. Making his way quickly out of the church he stood gratefully in the heavy warm air. The girl followed him, hesitated, then sat on a tomb, a massive block like a solid table. Tony waited a moment, then sat next to her. She disturbed him, but somehow he wanted to be with her, find out more about her.

'What's your name?' he asked.

'Ann.'

'Mine's Tony,' he offered.

'Yes, I know.'

Tony felt uncomfortable again.

'How do you know?' he asked.

'I've watched you. You're Tony, and your friends are George and Steve. That's what you call each other.'

The sensible, everyday explanation didn't calm Tony's unease. There was something about the girl that was strange, even without the Toad Lady. While they were talking she stared too closely at him, never taking her eyes away like you usually do when you're speaking. It unnerved him. He felt he was being tested and examined and he didn't know what for.

'You know the Toad Lady,' he said, deciding to try straight away to find out what she was doing.

'What?'

'The Toad Lady, you know her. We saw you the other day at her house in the woods.'

Understanding painted the girl's face.

'Miss Tasker.'

'I don't know. She's the Toad Lady.'

The girl laughed and for the first time Tony felt relaxed with her, but she fired a question at him before he could enjoy it.

'How old are you?'

'Eleven.'

'And I'm ten,' she said.

'Do you go to that school?' she asked, pointing at Mrs Hodgson's house with the classrooms next to it.'

'I did, but I've left. Next term I'm going to the school in town, with Steve.'

'What about George?'

'No, he's staying here, he's ten.'

'But he's bigger than you.'

'He's big, but he's only ten.'

The girl nodded.

'Where do you live?' Tony asked her.

She told him, but he had never heard of it.

'Don't you live here now?'

'No. I've come to stay with Miss Tasker for a while.'

Tony gaped.

'You're living with the Toad Lady?'

She nodded again. Usually, when Tony met people, they tried to help you to understand them, they wanted to explain themselves, but this girl didn't seem to care. She said what she meant and left it to him to accept it or understand it for himself. She didn't explain or excuse. This was difficult for Tony.

'But don't you mind?' he asked.

'Mind?'

'Being out there in the woods, with her?'

She laughed again.

'Come and meet her,' she said.

Tony shook his head.

'Please. Come for tea?'

'Do you mean it?'

'Of course.' The grown-up deepness in her

voice made it real.

He thought.

'No.'

The girl's face fell. She slid off the tomb, he dress hitching up, showing very white legs before i dropped back into place. She had not spent he summer baking in the sun like the boys.

'Well, goodbye, then,' she said, and set of down the path.

'Hey,' he called, but she ignored him, a though he had stopped existing for her.

He dropped to the ground and set off after her Grabbing her scabbed elbow he swung her around catching her as she staggered.

'Don't go,' he said.

'I have to. It's time I was back.'

'I'll come to tea,' he said.

'Will you?'

'Yes. Yes, please.'

'Tomorrow, then.'

'All right.'

'I'll tell Miss Tasker to expect you.'

Tony couldn't believe that he nodded hi agreement, but he did.

'Come to the front gate, I'll be waiting.'

'All right.'

'Goodbye, Tony.'

'Bye, Ann.'

Tony was still in the graveyard looking down th

road, when George and Steve skidded up the dusty path on their bikes.

'Come on,' they yelled, and flung themselves on top of him, banging his head against the blockish tomb where he had sat with Ann.

'You clowns,' he shouted.

They rolled on the grass, hooting with laughter, Steve pulling thick handfuls of it away from the dry earth. The sparse juice stained his hands as he crushed the stalks and jammed them prickly down Tony's neck.

'Get off. Get off,' he wriggled and squealed, but George planted his thighs over Tony's chest while Steve filled his shirt with grasses.

'Thought we'd forgotten you?' asked Steve.

'No, no, no,' George insisted.

'All right. I give up. Get off,' Tony begged.

Steve and George let their eyes meet to check that they agreed, then George rolled off and lay on his back, hands behind his head. Steve sat, leaning his back against the tomb. Tony panted after his struggle and tried to smile at them.

'Thought we'd forgotten you, didn't you?' Steve repeated.

'No.'

'Yes you did.'

'I was just keeping cool,' Tony explained.

'Too hot,' agreed Steve.

'Right,' said George.

'Not cool here at all,' Steve carried on.

'I was in the church,' Tony insisted. 'I've only just come out.'

'On your own, were you?' Steve asked, as though he knew something.

The slight hesitation gave Tony away.

'Yes.'

George and Steve did an odd thing. They didn't look at each other.

'Well, we're here now, to keep you company.'

'Yes,' agreed Tony.

'Want to go down Fletcher's?'

'I don't think so.'

'The railway line. Squash some coins?'

Tony shook his head.

'Like it here?' asked Steve persistently.

'Yes.'

'All right, then. We'll play in the church. Come on.'

Steve stood up, and George sprang to his feet.

'Come on.'

Tony remembered the row when he had frightened Steve in the church. He didn't like what was happening. He made no move.

'Are you coming?' Steve asked.

'Yes. Coming?' George was unusually positive.

'I don't know.'

'Come on. We're going in.'

Tony had always liked being alone in the church, liked the feeling of strangeness it gave him, and he didn't very much like messing around in there. Now, although the girl had made him shiver with her talk about the old-time woman's eyes staring up through the centuries, he more than ever didn't want to go in with George and Steve, didn't want to disturb whatever it was that was in there.

George stood over him, smiling.

Tony nodded, stood up, and followed.

'We've got this great idea,' Steve called over his shoulder as he pushed open the huge door. His voice was caught by the hollow claws of the church and twisted into a nervous cackle.

Tony knew that this was going to be bad, but he stepped in, trapped.

7

In the Book

The Toad Lady smiled at the girl as she came in through the front door. Outside, the goat baahed sadly. He liked company, and the girl always stopped to pet him on her way in; but he was never satisfied with a few strokes and always wanted her to go on and on, scratching his head and tickling his ears. She soon grew tired of petting him and went in.

'He's bleating for you,' said the Toad Lady.

'Oh, dear. I'm sorry.'

'Never mind. I suppose it's better to have a few strokes than none at all.'

'Don't you ever stroke him?' the girl asked.

'Me? I've got more things to do than stand in the garden stroking a giddy goat.'

The Toad Lady was pouring boiling water over large, crinkled tea leaves that opened up as they soaked. They were in a large room, more than half the size of the ground floor of the house. The floor had an uneven, red-tiled pattern, with some rush mats dotted here and there. There were a couple of comfortable chairs at one end with a dining table and chairs by the window. At the other end of the room was a pottery sink, a few cupboards and a fridge and a cooker. It didn't look like any particular sort of room at all; not a kitchen, it was too homely and comfortable for that; not a dining-room, it was too rambling for the idea of formal meals; not really a living-room because of the evidence of cookery and food preparation, but more of a living-room than anything else.

There were large bunches of wild flowers and herbs dangling from hooks in the ceiling, and these filled the room with an aroma of the fields and meadows. Jars of fresh flowers from the garden, roses and pinks, tiger-lilies and dahlias, were on the table and the mantlepiece, wherever there was a space for them. The boundary between indoors and outdoors seemed to have been broken down, and it would not have been a surprise if the room were carpeted with turf instead of the red tiles.

Ann had grown used to watching as the Toad Lady moved through this space like a magician. She arranged the flowers, tied up the bunches, prepared the food, slicing vegetables quickly with a fierce sharp knife; she tipped portions of food into scalding water, stirred pans, mixed ingredients in a dark brown earthenware bowl; and all the time she kept up a stream of chants and incantations, filling

the air with hot smells from her pans and deep rhythmic tunes from her throat.

Just now, all she was arranging was a tray with two mugs for hot tea and two plates for fresh scones from the oven.

The girl watched, half-absorbed in the activity and half-distracted by a blue Persian cat that sprang lazily on to her lap and stretched out to be fondled.

Neither the Toad Lady nor the girl spoke to each other for a while, until the tea had infused and was ready to be tipped through the strainer into the mugs. Then the Toad Lady sat opposite the girl and smiled again. She made some mysterious movements with her hands, like the ones the boys had seen, but the girl frowned and shook her head.

'All right,' said the Toad Lady, 'you look tired. I'll give you an afternoon off.'

The girl smiled back.

'Thank you.'

They drank their tea in silence for a moment, crumbs from the fresh scones dropping on to their plates. Then the girl looked shyly at the woman.

'Miss Tasker?'

'Yes.'

'May I ask you a question?'

'Of course.'

'I don't mean to be rude.'

'I'm sure you don't, Ann. What is it? Is there something wrong?'

'No. But.'

'Yes?'

'Well, why do they call you the Toad Lady?'

The woman paused, with her mug half-way to her mouth, then she lowered it as if to free her hand to reach out and slap the girl, or curl her fingers into a position to curse her.

'The Toad Lady?'

'Yes.'

She finally let go of her mug, and roared with laughter.

Inside the church, the boys stood quietly.

'I don't want to,' said Tony.

'I told you, didn't I?' Steve said to George.

'That's right,' he agreed. 'You said so.'

'I'm not frightened,' Tony argued.

'Course you are.'

'Not.'

'Well, if you're not, you'll do it.' Steve concluded.

'Look, I don't want to. If I wanted to I would, and I wouldn't be frightened, but I don't want to. All right?'

'I suppose,' Steve said slowly, 'that if you play with girls you start to get frightened. That's right, isn't it George?'

'That's right.'

'What do you mean?' demanded Tony.

'I mean that you used to play with us, didn't you? And when you played with us you were all

78

right. But now you play with girls and you act like a girl, don't you?'

Tony shouted.

'You been spying? Have you? You been hiding in corners and watching me?'

'Don't need no hiding,' said Steve. 'Do we George?'

'No hiding needed,' agreed George.

'Just come over the fields from the railway and see you. That's all we need to do. Playing in the churchyard with the girls.'

Tony wanted to deny it, wanted to say that he'd only been speaking to the girl, wanted to get Steve and George to like him again. He thought he might say how he'd found her looking at the old-time lady and the way she talked. That would make them laugh. Tony was good at making them laugh. He thought that was why George and Steve liked him, even though he didn't like fighting like they did, or getting bruised and dirty.

'Perhaps you'd like to play with her dolls?' Steve taunted him.

Should he? Should he tell them about her? He thought he could do a fair imitation of her voice, deep and slurred. Then he could tell the story, making fun of how she sounded when she said the odd things about the old-time lady.

'He could tuck them up in bed,' George agreed. This was very shaming. George never thought of things like that to say, only Steve did.

79

He remembered the girl, her invitation to him, and the way she went off when he said no. He remembered that he had said he would go to tea. George and Steve looked at him, waiting.

They were standing by a table at the church door. There was a visitors' book open on it, with the names of people who had stopped to come in and look at the church.

'Go on, then,' Steve said.

'All right,' agreed Tony, keeping silent about the girl. Somehow, he didn't want to betray her.

'Her name's Nelly,' Steve said.

'We don't know that. Not really.'

'Yes it is. C.N. Hodgson.'

The boys always called Mrs Hodgson 'Nelly' when they were wanting to be rude about her. If she had been particularly fierce or nasty to one of them, if she had written something scathing on a piece of work they'd done, then it was always, 'Old Nelly Hodgson did it.'

'That could be anything,' Tony argued. 'We'll just put her initials.'

'That's no good,' Steve insisted. 'It has to be Nelly.'

Tony gave in. He picked up the pen next to the book and he wrote in the column headed, *Name*, 'Old Nelly Hodgson'.

George and Steve hugged each other when they saw it. George pretended that he was going to pee in his trousers it was so funny, and Steve

stamped his feet so hard he hurt his toe. Even Tony had to admit that it looked very funny.

'Oh dear,' gasped Steve, holding his sides.

'The address,' said George. 'You've got to put the address.'

'No, that's enough,' Tony argued.

'No. Go on. Go on.' Steve urged him. Then he whispered something in Tony's ear.

'No,' said Tony, shocked.

'Yes. Go on.'

'What?' asked George. 'What is it?'

'You wait,' said Steve. 'Go on.'

Tony wrote in the next column.

'School House Toilet.'

George ran right up the centre of the church, shrieking. Steve pushed his handkerchief into his mouth, tears running down his cheeks. Tony looked at what he had written, and began to think it wasn't funny any more. He had disguised his writing to look like someone else's, but it didn't look like any of the other entries in the book. The letters were large and well-formed, not like the irregular scrawl of grown-ups'.

'Come on,' shouted Steve, and tore out of the church.

Tony was next, with George last through the door. George and Steve grabbed their bikes while Tony watched.

'Get on,' George shouted, and Tony hopped his leg over the crossbar.

George's strong legs powered the bike along, and the boys didn't speak until they got to the ford.

'Good old Tony,' said Steve, when they lay on the bank alongside Fletcher's.

'Yeah,' agreed George.

Now that they were well away from the terrible words written in the book it was no longer as funny, nor as frightening. It was only in the church that there was danger.

'What if they find out?' asked Tony, who still hadn't gained the casual ease about the crime that the others seemed to feel.

'They can't,' said Steve.

'Why not?'

'Because we were all there. We know what happened.'

'So?' Tony was not convinced.

'Well, if they ask us who it was, we just say we don't know. If we all say the same, they can't do anything, can they?'

'I suppose not,' agreed Tony.

'That's right,' said George, who was saying more this summer than he ever had before; something had happened to George.

'What's she like?' asked Steve suddenly.

'What?' said Tony.

'The girl,' said Steve. Then he did a funny thing. He lowered his voice a little and said, 'Don't knock me over, I'll cry,' in quite a good imitation of her.

Tony felt again the strange feeling he had had before, of being light-headed and slightly sick, as though his stomach was not right. He didn't answer Steve.

'Well?'

'What?'

'What did she say to you?'

'Nothing really.'

'Come on. Tell us. Is she coming to live round here?'

'I don't know.'

'You must.'

'No, she's not. Not for ever. I think she's staying with someone.'

'Who?'

George was listening, but not taking any part in the conversation, more like his old self.

'I don't know.'

'Where?'

'She didn't say.'

Steve began to sound annoyed.

'You didn't find out much.'

'She said she didn't mind you knocking her over.'

'Why did she run away then?'

'You surprised her, she said. Took her by surprise.'

'No reason to run away.'

'Well, you were running away,' Tony pointed out.

'Pardon?'

'Running away. If anyone was, you were.'

Steve looked the other way.

'Just running,' he said at last. 'Not running away.'

'Oh.'

'Yes.'

'That's right,' George agreed.

Tony stared.

'But you were there,' he said. 'You . . .'

'That's right,' George nodded. 'I was there. Steve was just running. Not running away.'

Steve stood up.

'Time for my tea,' he announced, picking up his bike. 'See you tomorrow,' he added to Tony.

'Oh, yes.'

'We'll go to the railway line tomorrow afternoon, shall we?'

'I don't know,' answered Tony.

'Three o'clock,' said Steve. 'I'll come round for you at three.'

The two bikes made small skid marks in the dust as they shot off.

'Three o'clock,' George called over his shoulder.

Back at the Toad Lady's house the girl made the arrangements for Tony's tea.

8

Throwing Sticks

The huge horse-chestnut tree spread its green arms wide, the broad bright leaves hanging flatly, filtering the sun. Underneath, the boys' faces stared up, stained with the ghostly light. George and Steve were hurling dead branches into the tangled knots of the tree, pelting them against the high conkers hidden in the foliage. They clattered against the trunk, sometimes lodging there and refusing to come down, sometimes dragging bits of twig and leaf with them as they dropped to the ground. The conkers, still green and juicy in their shells, clung victoriously to the stems, refusing to budge.

'Not ready yet,' Tony said, as he joined them.

Steve grunted.

'Time they were,' he said. 'I'm ready for them.'

'They aren't any good anyway if you get them down while they're still green.'

'I know,' Steve replied, not looking at Tony. He picked up a blunt log, weighed it carefully,

eeling its balance and shape, then he took aim at
a cluster of larger conkers fairly low down, and sent
t spinning with a deadly grace through the leaves.

The log bit at the group and dislodged two
conkers. They banged their way through the green-
ry plunging to earth.

Steve grabbed them triumphantly.

'Got some,' he yelled to George, who was now
rying to scramble up the trunk. The trunk was too
vide for handholds, and there were no low-lying
ranches to use as grips.

Tony watched Steve squeeze the shells between
is palms. The spikes stuck into him. Tony would
ave cried out in pain and dropped it, but Steve
crewed up his face and carried on pressing.

When the conkers were ripe, they fell readily
rom the crisp, brown husks, but there were still
everal weeks of sun needed to bring those to
eadiness. Juice oozed from the fruit and stained
teve's hands. He dropped the shell and swore,
ooking at the tiny pricks on his palms. Stamping on
he conker he sent it spinning off up the road. He
an after it and snatched it up. It had split open,
howing creamy white flesh and a milky centre that
till had to be baked hard and brown. He swore
gain, and threw it far over the fence into the field.

'Never ready when you want them,' he said.
Then, when they are, you're fed up, or they all
ome at once, and shrivel up before you can use
hem.'

Tony thought of how they would go out late and fill their pockets with them – dozens and dozens, shiny, marbled, smooth bodies with a rough scar at the top. More than they would ever use. More than they could ever play with.

They picked up their bikes and rode to the shop. Eating ice lollies with one hand and guiding the wheels with the other, they rode through the village, not looking for anything, not planning, just glad to be there.

The summer had streched out long and ho before them, but now was drawing to its close.

'Eleven days,' said George.

'What's that?'

'Eleven days and I go back to Old Nelly.'

'Oh, yes.'

'And you go off to the grammar.'

Steve agreed. The grammar was the schoo they all went to when they left the little villag school. Once, only people who passed an exam went there, but that had all changed and now everyone did, though it was still called the grammar school for some reason.

They all thought about the new term, but said nothing.

A bus, hired by the School, drove through al the villages, picking up people for the grammar. I eleven days time, George would walk on his own up the lane to the little classroom and Old Nelly Hodgson, and Tony and Steve would put on their new uniform for the first time and get on the bus together. George would still be free in his own village, but Steve and Tony would be carried off, prisoners; but they would be together and George would be in solitary confinement, the last of the group.

Tony thought hard before he spoke.

'I can't come this afternoon,' he said.

'Where?'

George had forgotten, but Steve remembered.

'But we're all going,' he said. 'Down the railway line.'

'I can't. I'm doing something else.'

The bikes whirred in the background to their conversation, and Steve and Tony had to adjust their speeds to keep on talking to each other.

'Oh, yes?'

'Where you going?' George asked.

'Doesn't matter.'

Tony drove his pedals down hard, pulling away from the others. They attacked their bikes and sped after him. He rode quickly past the churchyard and dropped down the hill the other side.

They were panting when they got to the ford.

'Look,' shouted Tony. 'It's gone.'

It had. The boys had never seen it completely dry before. A tiny dribble of water went through the cutting under the road, but the main flow over the tarmac had dried up, leaving a mark where it had crawled.

'Going with your girlfriend?' Steve asked.

'What?'

'You heard.'

'Girlfriend?' said George.

'That one in the graveyard. You know.'

George grinned, stupidly.

Tony spoke very quietly.

'I can't come this afternoon.'

Steve dropped his voice to the deep, slurred sound of the girl's.

'Oh, Tony. I love you.'

George thought for a second, then he laughed.

'Oh, Tony,' he repeated, with none of Steve's success in imitation.

'Shut up.'

Steve laughed too.

'Won't you leave those rough boys. Come and play with me.'

Steve pursed his lips and made a kissing sound.

Without a word, Tony went and stood over Steve where he lay sprawled.

'Oh, Tony.'

Tony heaved his foot and kicked Steve hard in the stomach.

'Here,' yelled George, and pulled him away.

Steve was gasping for breath, holding his middle.

'You can't do that,' George said.

'You hit him. You hit him all the time,' shouted Tony.

'That's different.'

Steve found his feet and threw himself at Tony. They were evenly matched in size, and George backed away.

Tony quickly got the worst of it. After that first kick in rage he didn't want to hit Steve, he couldn't really let go at him. But Steve didn't seem to mind. His fists punched at Tony again and again, first in his stomach, doubling him up, then at his face until Tony dropped to the ground and lay there.

'That'll do,' said George. 'He's had enough.'

Tony waited, hoping that Steve had finished. There was blood flowing from his nose, and his eye was closing.

Steve swung a foot lazily against him, finding his stomach, but it was a false revenge, with no venom. He had had enough of hurting Tony, who didn't want to fight back.

'Give her a nice kiss,' he shouted, as he pushed his bike along the road, getting up speed to hop on and pedal away. George followed him closely.

After a while, Tony limped painfully away from the dry road, and found the trickle of Fletcher's in the trees. He bathed the blood from around his nose, and he soaked his handkerchief so that he could hold the comforting coolness to his swelling eye.

At dinner, his mother gave him a look, but she didn't comment on his bruised face. His jaw stabbed pains across his face when he chewed and it took him a long time to eat, but he finished everything rather than invite a question.

Afterwards he lay upstairs on his bed until it was time to go to meet the girl. His room was small and stuffy in the heat, and he didn't have his own radio or a television like some people he knew. Usually he read, but his closed eye gave him some trouble and he couldn't make the letters stand still. He gave up and lay on his back with his hands behind his head, as he did when he made the church tower fall on him.

In the afternoon heat even the birds seemed to have given up trying to sing; the farmers were not working in the fields nearby so there was no clatter of iron from them; only the insects were untroubled by the heat and kept up their humming and clicking and whistling, unless the noises were coming from right inside his battered head. There was a funny light feeling in there that made Tony think the noises might be inside him.

After splashing more cold water from the tap over his face, Tony made his way on foot down the hill to the ford and then through the tunnel of trees along Fletcher's.

Hidden behind the wall, Steve and George waited for Tony to arrive. They had been watching the house for days now, and were sure the girl was staying there. The goat browsed the meadow around the house. Inside, the girl and the Toad Lady pottered about preparing tea, the Toad Lady cool and unconcerned, the girl jumpy and nervous.

'He's only coming for a cup of tea,' said the Toad Lady.

'You won't mention it will you? Please,' begged the girl.

'It?' The Toad Lady raised her eyebrows.

'The Toads.'

She laughed, and stroked the girl's hair.

'We'll see what sort of a boy you've made a friend of.'

Tony stopped at the bend in the brook where he had to set off for the Toad Lady's house. There was a proper path off the main road and down to the garden wall, but that was a long way round. Approaching from the thicket made the house more mysterious, and didn't help him to come up to it with confidence.

Steve gripped George's arm as he heard Tony's feet breaking through the undergrowth. He inclined his head in the direction of the tread, and George nodded.

The Toad Lady touched the girl's arm when she heard Tony's knock on the door.

'He's here,' she said when the girl turned her face to her.

'Oh.'

'It's all right. I'll behave.'

'Thank you,' said the girl, and then realised that perhaps that wasn't the right answer. 'I mean. I don't mean you . . .'

'I know what you mean, and it's all right.'

'Thank you.'

The Toad Lady gave another smile.

'Let him in, then.'

Steve and George peered over the wall, taking care to keep themselves nearly hidden.

'He's going in,' said George.

'I wouldn't,' said Steve. 'Not in there. Not with the Toad Lady.'

Tony felt exactly the same as he knocked at the door. He wished he was anywhere else, but he had to go, especially after the way Steve had made fun of the girl, and especially after he had promised when she had walked away from him. He wanted to see the girl again, but he didn't want to have tea with the Toad Lady.

The door opened and the girl stood in the doorway.

'Come in.'

'She's going to poison him,' said George.

'Serve him right. I'm glad.'

Steve didn't like Tony at all since he'd kicked him.

Tony looked around the large room. He stood awkwardly, not knowing what to do. The Toad Lady was waiting for him, solemnly.

'This is Miss Tasker,' the girl introduced her.

'How do you do,' Steve said.

'Hello,' Her reply was bright enough, and she was less threatening than he remembered. If anything she was short and dumpy.

'And this is Tony.' The girl was very proper in her manners, her odd voice sounding even more like a grown-up's as she carried out the social formalities.

The Toad Lady put out her hand to Tony.

'We've met before, I think,' she said.

The girl flashed her a warning look.

'Do you like flowers?' asked the Toad Lady.

Tony felt stupid and clumsy.

'I don't know.'

'Don't know?' the girl asked.

'Now then, Ann.' The Toad Lady did a strange thing; she tapped the girl's shoulder before she spoke, so that the girl was looking at her. 'That's no way to talk to a guest. We've got to behave ourselves, haven't we?'

The girl frowned and made no answer.

'You don't do the garden at home, then?' the Toad Lady asked Tony, ignoring Ann.

'Not much.'

'So you wouldn't know about flowers, would you. No reason why you should.'

Tony was grateful to her for letting him off the hook of his ignorance.

'I don't suppose you do the altar flowers in that church you're always hanging around in.'

Outside, Steve and George watched and waited.

9

Old Spells

Inside the church the brass lady lay flat and cool under her scrap of rug. The eyes that had looked upwards for so many hundred years were blinded with the coarse fibres of the backing. Sun had forced more moisture from its stone prison and the air hung damp and heavy. Small, indifferent snaps and creaks burst meaninglessly from the oak pews and panels as they adjusted to the humidity. The lone hand of the clock crawled around its face, coming to the Roman IIII with a click that made wheels inside begin to move and spin, dragging the small hammer sharply over the bell. One, two, three, four, tolled hollowly through the nave. Mrs Hodgson, the headmistress, straightened her back, stopped dusting and checked the time against her watch. Time to go, put the kettle on. She stood slowly so that she should not feel dizzy or fall. Getting up used to be so easy, a quick leap and there you were; now, a sudden movement to the upright was dangerous. She tidied the pile of magazines by the door on the way out, and her eye fell on the entries in the Visitors' Book. For several seconds she paused, then lowered her head and squinted again, missing her spectacles. She closed the book, placed it under her arm and left the church.

The clock struck. One, two, three, four, strode over the fields in half-league boots, stamped on the two figures in the walled orchard of the Toad Lady's garden and marched on. Tony lifted his head at the echoes and looked in the direction of the church, but Ann paid no attention to the ringing.

They were sharing a book, brightly illustrated and well-used. It was lying open on the dry grass and they kept darting off and then returning to it. In their hands they carried small bundles of cane transformed into makeshift flags with scraps of notepaper at their tops. Several of these flags were driven into the ground and names written on the paper. Each one marked a different wild flower from the book that was growing in the wild garden. Tony was astonished to see how many there were already. 'Whatever you do, just mark them with a flag. Don't pick them,' the Toad Lady had warned. 'Some of them are getting very rare.' Tony pointed to a picture in the book, took Ann over to a distant part of the garden and looked questioningly at her. She shook her head and said, 'No, too big.'

Behind the wall, Steve and George scurried

about, building up an arsenal of missiles.

'Look,' Steve grinned. He turned out his pockets and a pile of green conker husks tumbled to the ground. George nodded and blew out his cheeks. He trotted off and came back with his hands cupped together. A heap of smooth, round stones joined the conkers.

Steve frowned. 'Not stones,' he whispered. 'Stones can hurt too bad.'

George sniffed. 'Only little 'uns.'

But Steve insisted. 'No stones.'

'No more conker trees here,' George argued. 'Need more than that.'

'Sticks,' suggested Steve.

George trotted off again like an obedient dog and this time he returned with an armful of sticks, about a foot long, as thick as his wrist.

'I dunno,' Steve thought.

George ignored him. 'More,' he said. And together they went off for more. Soon there was quite a pile of sticks and conkers.

Steve peered over the wall. Tony and Ann had their backs to him, absorbed in their search. He drew back his arm and lobbed a conker over. He used no force. It was just a placing shot, to get the range right. It fell uselessly far to the right.

Tony turned his head to see what had made the disturbance in the hedge. Steve ducked down and waited. He knew Tony would look all around before he went back to his game.

George breathed heavily and went pink trying to keep quiet. They put their heads above the wall together. Steve's arm was educated now and he weighed a conker in his hand, drew back and hurled it fast and hard with a swift flick of his wrist.

It landed just in front of the book, bounced, skidded, and dragged across the pages, tearing them.

Tony sprang to his feet. Ann looked round in surprise.

A stick soared over the wall and caught Tony on the leg.

'Quick! Duck!' he shouted.

Ann looked at the torn page, then up at Tony, wonderment in her face.

He grabbed her arm and dragged her to her feet. Sticks and conkers flew at them in a steady barrage. Tony stopped, picked up a conker and hurled it swiftly back, but he was off-balance and unprepared and it went far wide of the target.

Ann was smiling with pleasure.

'No!' he shouted, as though raising his voice would help her to understand. 'No! It's not a joke. Come on.'

A stick bounced off the goat's back and it bleated in pain.

Tony called out. 'Stop it. You pigs. Cowards.'

'Toad eater,' Steve's voice soared across the garden. 'Toady.'

Tony swore at him, looking wildly round for

somewhere to shelter from the hail of missiles. He picked up a green conker and poised himself to throw, swearing again at the top of his voice.

Three things happened at the same time, in slow motion, as though a film was running at half speed.

The Toad Lady appeared in the doorway of the

house, just in time to hear him swear richly at Steve and George.

She watched Tony pull back his arm and fling the conker.

Another conker curled its way through the air from behind the wall. It caught Ann full on the side of her face just below the left eye. She gasped, and flicked her head, too late.

Steve and George dropped out of sight below the wall and skirted the perimeter, away from the origin of the throw, arms full of missiles.

Ann's hand went to her face and came away stained with blood that the spikes from the unripe husk had dragged from her cheek. Tony was away at once and raking the top of the wall with his eyes. Ann, shaking, drew alongside him.

'What happened?' she asked.

Tony knew but was too ashamed to say. He caught a movement in the corner of his eye and swung around. At that moment George and Steve broke cover and stood up, pelting them with sticks and conkers and abuse. In the excitement their aim lost its accuracy and all the shots went short or wide, but Ann was frightened and moved nearer to Tony, gripping his side. This infuriated Steve more and he shouted louder and more fiercely.

'Girly. Girly. Playing with the flowers.'

A huge voice boomed out. 'The next boy to throw anything over my land will have me to answer to.'

The missiles stopped abruptly. The Toad Lady covered the ground from the door to the two children as though she had sprinted rather than made her usual determined stride. Steve and George dropped out of sight.

'Don't think you've got away with this,' she called to the empty air. 'I'll be seeing you soon, and we'll get some answers from you.'

Ann reached her hand out to the Toad Lady and let her take it.

'Come on,' she said, leading her to the house. Tony watched them go, his head bent, ashamed of his friends, ashamed of himself for bringing this attack to this house. He watched them, the broad, strong back of the Toad Lady and the slim white back of Ann and he felt sick in his stomach to be so alone, pelted by the boys from his school and abandoned by these strange people who had begun to show him such interesting new things. Lonely, tears pricked against the corners of his eyes. He was responsible for this trouble, for the rotten language hurled over the old wall and for the cruel cuts on Ann's face. He shrugged his shoulders and turned.

'Come on,' the Toad Lady shouted over her shoulder. 'I hope you're on our side in this. Bring the book in, will you?'

Tony lifted his head shyly and saw a fierce grin on her face. 'Good lad,' she shouted. He grinned back, darted to the book, swept it up in a single grab and sprang into the house after her.

10

Silent World

Inside, the Toad Lady sat Ann down, pulled a sprig of something from a bunch of herbs hanging from a hook on the ceiling rafters and scalded it with water from the kettle.

'That'll be ready in a minute,' she said, 'like tea, it needs a bit of time to make.'

While it was brewing she bathed the cuts on Ann's cheek with a wet cloth.

'You'll live,' she decided. 'Hold this against your face. Does it hurt?'

Ann nodded.

'All right. Well done.' She stroked Ann's hair and smiled at her. 'That gone green and cloudy yet?' she asked Tony. He nodded. The Toad Lady strained it off into a basin and threw away the herb. Tony thought of the poison and the toads. The mixtured looked like liquid toad, browny-green. She took a fresh piece of cloth, soaked it in the potion and applied it to the cuts. Ann didn't flinch at all.

'Much kinder than your antiseptics,' said the Toad Lady, 'and just as good. This'll stop it going septic and it'll keep away any swelling.'

Ann smiled at her. The blood had stopped and the only sign of the injury now was a pattern of three small stripes across her cheek.

'Looks like you could have done with some of this,' said the Toad Lady to Tony. She had not mentioned the cuts and bruises on his face before, and he had been grateful, but now that Ann was in a mess it didn't seem as bad.

'Look, I'm sorry,' he said. 'It's my fault this happened.'

'No it's not,' she said in a stern voice, but not unkindly. 'Do you want some?'

'What is it?' he asked warily.

'Betony.'

He scrunched up his nose.

'Just a herb,' she said. 'Then, in a fiercer voice. 'Though I don't know why I say, "Just a herb".'

Tony was amazed at the sudden shift of temper.

'Oh, it's all right,' she said. 'It's me I'm cross with, not you.'

'But why?'

'Why what?'

'Why are you cross.'

'I'm not cross,' said the Toad Lady. 'Not a bit.'

Tony wanted to give up. She was as changeable

and unhelpful as all grown-ups, after all.

'What I mean is,' she expanded. 'If I were to be cross, then I'm the person to be cross with. Not you. But I'm not cross, anyway. See?'

Tony did not see at all, so he nodded.

'You see, I use herbs for everything – cooking, medicine, making things smell nice. I even use them to keep ants out of the pantry. They're marvellous. So, I'm sort of cross with myself for apologizing for them. They're not just herbs. They ARE herbs. And very powerful they are. Now, this is betony and it would take all of the sting and pain out of that eye of yours if you want to. Do you?'

Tony was far from sure, but he did not like to refuse. It seemed cowardly, with Ann sitting there with the betony compress on her cheek.

'All right,' he agreed.

The Toad Lady's hands were surprisingly gentle as she bathed his eye, and the potion felt cool and soothing.

'You've been in a fight,' she said.

Tony nodded.

'With them?'

'Yes.'

'I thought they were your friends.'

'They are. I mean, I think, that is, I thought . . .'

'Don't worry,' said the Toad Lady. 'There. That's done. Feel better?'

'Yes.'

'It won't stop the bruise coming out, but it'll stop it hurting so much.'

'Thank you.'

'I know about friends,' she said, going back in the conversation. 'And it's not that odd.'

'Isn't it? asked Tony.

'Not a bit. Nothing as funny as people. Don't like them much myself. Toads are nicer, I think.' She gave a funny, shy sort of smile when she said this and let her eyes go sideways to Ann to check with her, as though she'd said something naughty. But Ann was holding her head at an angle trying to keep her eyes on each of them during this quick chatter.

'Sorry,' said the Toad Lady, looking directly at her, 'we're leaving you out of this, aren't we. I'm to blame, going on at Tony.'

Ann smiled her thanks as Tony and the Toad Lady turned and faced the girl. They carried on their conversation, looking only at her without glancing at each other. Whenever the Toad Lady spoke or Ann answered they kept up a pantomime of hand movements and signals, like the ones Tony and the others had seen through the window the day they saw them learning to cast spells. They had not done this over tea and Tony felt very strange when they started.

'Tony's been having some fights,' explained the Toad Lady.

'I can see that,' said Ann.

106

'Well you're both in good company,' the Toad Lady replied.

'What was it about?' Ann asked.

Tony didn't answer.

'Was it me?' asked the Toad Lady.

'Sort of.'

'But not just me?'

Tony didn't answer.

'They don't like me, do they?' she said.

'No.'

Ann had her face screwed up in concentration and looked hard at Tony and then at the Toad Lady as they spoke, as though she was trying to get a picture of them in her mind.

'They're frightened of me?'

Tony nodded.

'But you're not?'

'No. Not any more.'

The Toad Lady looked pleased and Tony wasn't sure whether it was because George and Steve were frightened or because he wasn't.

'Frightened that I'll tell their mothers?'

Tony laughed. 'No, they wouldn't care about that.'

'Would you?'

Tony nodded and Ann grabbed the silence.

'But how could they be frightened of you?' she asked the Toad Lady.

'People are frightened of anything strange, anything they don't understand. I don't think those

107

boys know me like you do. Do they?' she asked Tony.

Ann didn't believe it and pestered Tony with other, silly questions, until he had to say what it was. He told her about seeing them, practising spells. When Ann laughed he wanted to get cross but he couldn't with the Toad Lady there.

'It's time to tell him,' she said to Ann. Ann objected but the Toad Lady insisted. Tony felt his stomach lurch – they were going to tell him about the spells. He wasn't sure that he wanted to know.

'Ann isn't like you and your friends. She's different.' Tony made no reaction, but sat and listened. He noticed Ann turn away from him so that her eyes were fixed directly on the Toad Lady. It was as though she couldn't bear him to discover about her. It made him more frightened than ever.

'You know that woman in the church?' the Toad Lady asked him. 'The brass one, lying, staring up into the silence?'

'Yes.'

'That's Ann.'

Tony wriggled, disbelievingly.

'I don't mean it's really her, that she stepped out from the brass. But that's what it's like for Ann. Silence, all around, always, everywhere.'

Ann still stared at her.

'You see,' the Toad Lady went on, 'Ann has to stare out at you, at me. She has to watch what we say, read it in our faces and on our mouths. That's her magic. And she can read it on my hands too. Or at least she's learning to. That's my magic.'

Ann looked to see how Tony was listening. Her face was beginning to lose some of its anxiety and she was starting to relax again. The streaks across her cheek were deepening and filling out to an angry red.

'There was a spell on her when she was born. There is on lots of people. Sometimes it makes them limp along rather than walk straight; sometimes they can't breathe without gasping and panting; sometimes it makes the world a blur in their eyes. There are lots of spells. You might say we all have spells cast on us when we're born. That's what makes us all different. With Ann, the spell closed her ears, made them useless. They poured plastic in them at the hospital and made moulds. They dangled wires from them to microphones to make the noise louder. But she was a baby and pulled the wires out and wouldn't wear the moulds. She learned to tell what we were saying by reading our lips.'

Tony interrupted the story.

'Was that how you knew our names?'

'That's right,' Ann grinned uncertainly. 'I didn't need to come near enough to hear you like anyone else, I could see what you were saying. I wasn't sure about George at first, I thought he was called John, they look alike on your lips.'

'But is it difficult?'

'I think it was better for me than for lots of people because I always did it, even when I was a baby and didn't know what talking was, I could tell by people's mouths whether they were being nice. The teachers taught me lots of new tricks and that helped, and once I knew what the words were and what your mouth looked like when you said them it was easy.'

'Is that why you talk funny?' he asked, and wished he hadn't.

'Do I?' she asked the Toad Lady. 'You said I didn't. You said it was all right.'

'It is all right,' she said, not looking angry with Tony although he felt he had done something terrible and she ought to be angry.

'Yes,' he said. 'It's fine. You just don't talk like we do round here.'

'Ann was lucky,' said the Toad Lady. 'The hearing aids were very good when she got old enough to leave them in, and that taught her what words sounded like so she could practise them, like all children do when they're growing up. She was a bit later than most, that's all.'

'That's right,' said Ann. 'And I still have lessons to make it sound right now, because I don't hear anything any more.'

'Why don't you wear the hearing aid then?' he asked. 'No one would mind.'

'I think Steve might,' Ann said. 'Don't you?'

Tony blushed.

'Don't tease him,' said the Toad Lady, but they all looked rather pleased to be saying something mean about Steve. Tony didn't understand how a grown-up could talk like this. 'Worse magic,' she carried on. 'This time Ann was attacked by dwarves, trolls, I don't know. Terrible things. They came and burrowed into her head, attacked her inside, scooped out the last bit of hearing that was left in her.'

Tony was getting used to the Toad Lady's strange way of talking. 'What was it really?' he asked. She grinned at him. 'Ann put up a good fight against them, but it took it out of her. She slept for weeks. Didn't have any strength left to wake up, it was all needed for the fight. She nearly died. But she won. She lost the last bit of hearing, but she's still alive. A few scratches from a conker aren't going to put her out after that.'

Tony looked at Ann again.

'Meningitis,' she said, forming the word perfectly. Tony had never heard of it, but he felt he understood. He could see the tiny armies fighting inside for control of her.

So Ann had come to stay in the village because the Toad Lady knew sign language and Ann wanted to learn it from her. She needed her special magic to fight the spell. They didn't teach it in her school any more, but Ann and her parents thought it would help her to know it. They found out about Miss Tasker who used to teach people with hearing difficulties before she came to the village.

Now Tony understood. He knew why Ann had not heard them running towards her out of the church; why she had not looked up when he found her looking at the brass lady; why she seemed to shut everything out once she turned her back on it, like the day she had asked him to tea and he had said no.

He sat back and looked round the kitchen, thinking again that it was the loveliest room he had ever been in – the smell of the herbs, the filtered light through the small windows, the rich red of the quarry tiles against the warm, veined wooden table and chairs, and the soft stroking of the breeze through the open door. He tensed all the muscles in his back, breathed deeply as though he could suck in the essence of the room and make it a part of himself, then relaxed.

The Toad Lady suddenly cried out and shattered his calm.

'I know,' she said. 'I know.' Ann of course could not tell how loud her voice was, but she could not miss the excitement in the quick movements and sudden activity.

Tony nervously wondered how soon he could make an excuse to leave. She was mad after all, quite mad. But the thought of walking out of the kitchen saddened him, and he hung on.

'Signs,' yelled the Toad Lady. 'We'll teach him some signs.'

'I'd better go,' said Tony. He stood up and wished he had a watch he could look at the way grown-ups did when they were pretending they had to be somewhere else. Ann was watching the Toad Lady, so she did not see him protest.

'Wonderful,' she said. 'That would be wonderful. Then he could talk to me and I wouldn't have to watch his lips all the time.' She laughed with pleasure.

Tony felt rather ashamed of himself.

'Well,' said the Toad Lady, sadly. 'If you've got to go.'

Ann saw her expression and looked at Tony with a puzzled expression. What was wrong?

'No,' he said. 'No, it's fine. I can stay. Really I can.'

The next hour was the maddest time he could ever remember. It was as though he had turned up at school only to find it had been taken over by a circus.

Miss Tasker stood Tony and Ann opposite one another. Then she would bark out a word, Ann would read her lips and make a sign. Then the word again, but this time Tony had to copy Ann.

'Woman,' she shouted, pointing to herself.

Ann lifted her right hand, the first finger pointing up. Then she stroked the side of the finger down her cheek.

'Woman,' repeated the Toad Lady. Ann repeated the action while Tony followed her.

'Good,' said the Toad Lady. 'See. Soft face. A woman. Terrible really, but it works. The next one's worse.' She mouthed at Ann, 'Man.'

Ann stroked her thumb and index finger over her chin.

'Man,' repeated the Toad Lady. Tony followed again.

'What's that?' the Toad Lady asked.

'Man,' he said.

She boxed his ears with such swift gentleness that he drew back alarmed. She laughed. 'Sorry. Won't hurt you. Bit of sign language, really.'

Tony gulped.

'No,' she went on. 'Why is it a man? Do it again.'

Tony stroked his thumb and forefinger down his chin again. It came to him. 'Beard,' he cried. 'I'm stroking a beard.'

'Good. Got it. Beard. Damn stupid, you see. But it works.'

Tony flushed with pride.

'Try this one,' she said. She made the sign for man again, then with her left hand she indicated a small person. Tony frowned.

Beard? Small person? He struggled.

'Come on,' she urged him. 'Work it out.'

Ann giggled.

'Dwarf,' said Tony.

The Toad Lady threw herself on to the floor and laughed. Ann grabbed her and demanded to know what was happening. Tony stood ashamed while the Toad Lady wrote 'DWARF' on Ann's hand. Ann shrieked and hugged the Toad Lady.

'Oh, I'm sorry.' she said, pulling Ann to her feet. 'I'm sorry. It's boy, you see.'

'Yes,' said Tony, carefully.

'Oh, you're cross now.'

'No,' he lied. But he was surprised that she bothered to say so. Grown-ups don't care whether children are cross or not. It makes no difference.

'Yes you are. And it's my fault. I am sorry. Please say it doesn't matter. You see . . .' but she could not finish what she was saying. A gust of laughter broke from her again. 'Dwarf,' she gasped helplessly. 'Oh, dear.'

Something about the apology had made Tony not care about the laughter and this time he joined in.

'You see,' she explained, when they had all finished. 'The system's supposed to be simple. And it is. You worked out that thing about the beard, all right. But then it breaks down. That sign meant man, but small man, that is a boy. But you thought it meant small man with beard – dwarf. It's obvious. Your answer's better than the real one. Don't you see?'

Tony nodded.

'Good lad,' she approved. 'Good lad.'

Tony nodded happily.

There were more shrieks of laughter through

all the rest of the lesson. Tony thought he had never laughed so much. So that when it really was time for him to go he hardly knew how to tear himself away.

'You'll come again, won't you?' said the Toad Lady, her voice steady and her face serious.

'Yes, please.'

'Tomorrow,' begged Ann. 'You'll come tomorrow?'

He looked at the Toad Lady.

'I'd like that,' she agreed.

As he left, the goat ambled across the grass towards him, hoping to be stroked. It was an affectionate goat.

'That's a nice boy you've met,' said Miss Tasker. Ann smiled at her.

11

Toad Flax

Overnight Tony's eye lost its red, puffy look. When he examined himself in the bathroom mirror the next morning he whistled with pleasure. It was half-closed and surrounded by a deep purple stain that started under the skin and welled up, overflowing onto his cheek.

'Great,' he said.

His mother was less happy.

'I'll be having something to say about this,' she said.

'Oh, no. Mum, please.' He begged her.

'Going around beating people up.'

'It's nothing.' But it was something. He was really proud of it. George and Steve got scuffs and bruises in their scuffles all the time, but he was more careful and never got marked except on his legs from falling off the bike. To have a real black eye was like wearing a medal. It meant he was tough.

'And what do *they* look like?' she asked. 'Did

you close their eyes for them? Did you? Are they walking about with great bruises on their faces? Time you learned to look after yourself.'

And so she took his medal away from him and gave him a shameful badge instead; the mark of the loser.

'And if you can't look after yourself I'll have to do it for you. I'll be having a word.' Her face was set and hard as she banged the dishes and plates about on the breakfast table.

'You can't.'

'Can't I just? Just you wait and see. Who was it?'

Tony kept quiet.

'That George? He's too big for his boots. Or your friend Steve? I've never liked him. That family were never any good. Which one was it?'

Still he was silent.

'I see,' she said, her mouth disappearing into a straight, thin line. 'Well, I'll have to go round and see both of them.'

Tony tensed his body and drove his fingernails into the palms of his hands.

'Please don't, Mum. Please. It doesn't matter.'

His mother saw his distress. It was hard for her to be two parents in one. Tony's father had died when he was only two. Now, she wanted to shout at him and hold him tight in her arms at the same time. She stretched painfully, trying to ease the tension that knotted a pain into her back.

119

'But, Tony, what am I to do? You can't get knocked about like this and do nothing about it, can you?'

'It was only a fight.'

'I know fights with boys,' she said, still firm but trying to be more gentle. 'They hit each other. One gets a black eye, the other gets a bruised cheek. Something like that. What did the other one get in this fight? Is his mother looking at him like I'm looking at you?'

· Tony looked down and mumbled. He looked so small, so hurt.

'Come on,' she said, more gently. 'What did you do to him, George or Steve or whoever?'

'Nothing.' Tony's voice was so low she could only just catch the word as it slipped shamefully from his lips.

'Nothing. That's right. So it wasn't a fight, was it? I don't mind boys fighting. It was a beating up.'

'No. No, it wasn't.'

'Well, tell me this then. Was it only one? Was it? Or were there two of them on to you at the same time?'

Tony remembered George backing off and letting Steve do it on his own. If he said there were two of them his mother would go round. If he said it was only one then he had clearly lost a fair fight.

'Just the one,' he said.

'And who started it?'

Who? Who made the fight, or who swung the

first kick?

'I did,' he mumbled.

His mother stood up and started to clear the things from the table. To Tony's relief she said, 'Then there's nothing I can do, is there? We're a fine pair, aren't we? You with that eye and me with this stupid back.'

Tony moved behind her and rubbed a hand slowly across her shoulders.

'Isn't there anything?' he asked. 'Anything to make it hurt less?'

'Wish there was,' she said. 'Nothing touches it. It's deep inside somehow.'

Tony remembered the kitchen with its red tiles, warm sunlight and bunches of herbs.

'I'd better go,' he said.

His mother nodded and squeezed his hand. 'No more fights?' she asked.

'No,' he agreed, ashamed for a moment of his medal.

She smiled, watched him leave the kitchen and wheel his bike up the path to the road.

The bike bumped along the rough track to the Toad Lady's house, and when the goat bleated at him Tony felt more anxious than ever. It was not fear this time, not fear of magic or spells or poisons, but real anxiety that they would not want to see him again. Perhaps she had meant to say something about the way he swore at George and Steve and had forgotten? Perhaps she had only been kind because she wanted to spare Ann embarrassment? Perhaps . . .

'I've got a present for you,' Ann called out as she opened the door.

Tony's face relaxed into a grin.

'That's a shiner,' said the Toad Lady, examining Tony's eye with what was astonishingly like approval.

'Doesn't hurt, though,' he said.

'Good.'

'Here,' said Ann. 'Look.'

It was a book. A big book. Tony had never had a book as old as this, never even held one. All his own books were paperbacks, or comic annuals. Even the books at school were all new. This was big and heavy and it did not have a picture on the front. It was bound in something thick and warm, with a dull red shine. Leather? The edges were grazed and the corners were broken and scuffed. He held out his hand, but Ann put the book down on the big, cluttered table and opened it.

Between the pages was a whole countryside of flowers. Not pictures, but real flowers, picked and pressed and dried between the pages. He gasped.

'You're not allowed to do that,' he protested.

'Good lad,' approved the Toad Lady.

Ann did not hear and kept turning the pages.

Tony looked at the Toad Lady in horror.

'It's all right,' she said. 'They're all very common. I collected them myself. But you're right to think that.'

'Here it is,' Ann pounced on a flat flower.

'They're beautiful,' Tony murmured as the colours flashed past.

Ann picked it up and handed it out to Tony. He was disappointed that it was only a flower after all. He had wanted to hold the book, to own it for himself, no matter what it was about. In its own way it was more beautiful than the flowers it held.

'Thank you,' he said with a serious face.

Ann laughed.

'Careful,' the Toad Lady warned her. 'Tony will think we're laughing at him again.

Tony, who was thinking exactly that, smiled and said, 'No. It's fine. I like coming here because you laugh so much. We don't laugh a lot at home.' He wished as soon as he had said it, that he hadn't.

He turned the flower over in his hands.

'Well?' demanded the Toad Lady, with her cross voice suddenly back. 'What is it?'

Ann laughed again.

The long stems and dark, five-pointed leaves were easy. It was ivy. But it had small purple flowers with yellow hearts. He shrugged.

'Come on,' she urged him.

'Ivy,' he said, knowing it was wrong.

'Wrong,' shouted Ann. 'Wrong.'

'Right,' the Toad Lady corrected her.

Ann scowled.

'Wrong,' she repeated.

'Right and wrong,' the Toad Lady conceded. 'Here,' she prodded a finger at the leaves. 'You see. Ivy leaves. Couldn't be anything else. Good.'

Tony swelled with pleasure.

'But you see the flowers. That's all wrong,' she went on. 'Tell him, Ann. It's your joke.'

Ann took a deep breath to stop herself giggling. 'It's Ivy-leaved toad flax,' she said.

Tony studied the flowers.

'I've never seen it,' he said.

'Seems she wanted to give you something to do with toads, for some reason,' said the Toad Lady. 'Lemonade?'

'Yes please.'

The lemon-juice mixture that she gave him was nothing like the stuff he had had from the village shop.

'I know,' she apologized. 'I make it myself from fresh lemons. You don't like it.'

Tony considered the polite lie that he thought his mother would probably want him to say. 'I might grow to like it,' he admitted truthfully.

'You do that,' she agreed. 'You do.'

'I really like the toad flax,' he assured Ann. 'Thanks a lot.'

'Right,' said the Toad Lady. 'Here you go. It grows in crevices.'

'What's a crevice?'

'A crack. A gap. And it likes water and shade and cool, damp, places.'

Tony put the expression on his face that he used when he was being told something at school which was going to be tested later.

'What's the matter?' demanded the Toad Lady roughly. 'Does that eye still hurt?'

'No. No,' he hastened to tell her. 'It's fine.'

'Just wondered,' she said, 'why you were pulling that face.'

Tony dropped his expression of concentration.

'Right,' she said. 'There's sure to be ivy-leaved toad flax somewhere in the village. See if you can find some. If you do, there's pudding after lunch. If you don't there isn't. All right?'

Tony and Ann agreed.

'Go on, then.'

They left Tony's bike and walked together down the side of the dry brook.

'Should be some round here,' Tony suggested. 'It's cool and damp.'

'Not really,' Ann pointed out. 'Not now. It's nearly as hot here as anywhere else.'

'That's true,' he admitted regretfully.

'Your face is a mess,' he said.

'What's that?'

'Your face is . . .' He turned to look straight at her and made sure he moved his lips a lot. 'Your face is a mess,' he repeated quietly but distinctly. He had forgotten. Her hand moved to her cheek and she ran the tips of her fingers along the marks. The wound was clear and fresh, but it was low and close to the cheek, not raised at all or swollen. Although it had not had a dressing on it there was no sign that it might become septic.

'Does it hurt?' Tony asked.

'No. Not at all. I think Miss Tasker's remedy worked.'

'It must've,' Tony agreed.

'You're a mess, too.'

'Oh, this. It doesn't matter.'

'I suppose boys are always getting black eyes.'

'Oh, a fair bit.' Tony spoke of his first black eye as though he had one delivered every week with his comic.

'Will it go soon?' she asked.

'About a week, I suppose. Longer than yours.'

'Miss Tasker said, if anyone asked, that I was to say she had turned into a cat and dragged her claws across my face to punish me for being cheeky.'

'She didn't?'

'Yes.'

'Does she always talk like that?'

'No. A lot of the time though.'

They broke clear of the stream and turned on to the path that led up to the village.

Tony looked around. There was no sign of Steve or George. As though she understood what he was anxious about Ann suggested, 'We could sit in the churchyard and think about it.'

'All right,' Tony agreed readily. He didn't

suppose they would want to go there at the moment, with the message in the visitor's book.

They found a spot round the back of the church, out of sight both of the road and of the school. The wall against their backs was deliciously cool after the fierce heat. Tony sucked a piece of sweet grass and looked up. Not a single cloud broke the deep blue of the sky.

'I liked that book,' he said.

Ann ignored him. He found it hard to believe that he could keep forgetting to look at her when he spoke. It was because she was so easy to be with. It was the first time he had had a friend who wanted to do more than just ride a bike and punch him.

He tapped her shoulder. 'I liked that book,' he said.

She nodded vigorously. 'It's perfect. It's all about flowers,' she said. And every real flower is pressed in the page that tells you about it.'

'Is it yours?'

'No. Miss Tasker's. She's had it years.'

Tony wanted to show that he had noticed that. 'Yes,' he said. 'It looks really old.'

Ann laughed. 'It is. Older than her. It's three hundred years old.'

'This is older,' he said, springing to his feet to cover his shame. He rubbed his hands over the wall they had leaned against. 'Nine hundred years old.' He dug his nails into the flaking mortar between the huge stones. It crumbled out.

'You'll pull it down,' Ann warned him. 'If you take all the cement out.'

'No,' he protested. He grabbed a handful of weed that had dug its roots into the mortar, pulled it out and dropped it to the ground.

'That's it,' Ann yelled. 'That's it!'

Tony whirled round and scanned the church-yard. 'What's up?' he asked. 'What's wrong?'

Ann picked up the weed. 'Ivy-leaved toad flax,' she said, brandishing it.

'Pudding,' said Tony. 'We'll have some pudding.'

They sprinted down the gravel path and through the village.

12

Mandrake

Pudding was better than he had dreamed it could be and Tony waited until he had eaten his second helping before he nerved himself up to ask Miss Tasker.

'Are there herbs for rheumatism,' he asked.

RHEUMATISM, she scribbled on Ann's hand so that she should not be left out.

'You haven't got rheumatism,' she squealed. 'Old people get that.'

The Toad Lady frowned.

'Devil's Claw,' I think,' she said, not writing the strange name on Ann's hand, a sure sign that she was not pleased with her.

'Have you?' Ann repeated.

'That's not a nice name for it,' said Tony. 'It's terrible in your hands.'

'It's not a name for rheumatism, it's a herb,' said Miss Tasker. 'And,' turning to Ann, 'no, he hasn't. But I bet his mum has.'

Smiling, Ann nodded at Tony who nodded back. He took her hand and wrote DEVIL'S CLAW on it while Miss Tasker crossed the kitchen and flung open the wooden door to a deep cupboard.

She rummaged round mumbling to herself. 'No. Not that. Ah, yes. Or, perhaps. No. No, again. Definitely not,' she decided of one jar, dropping it into the waste bin. 'Don't know what that's doing there at all.'

Tony marvelled at this constant stream of comment that Ann would never hear.

'Oh, gracious,' said Miss Tasker. 'Who'd have thought that was there?' She tucked something forked and withered under her arm and continued searching.

Tony and Ann waited. She returned to the table and tipped out her collection of packets, envelopes and small jars.

'Now then.' Fixing her half-rim spectacles on her nose she leafed through the pages of the huge book that Tony had loved so much the first time he had seen it.

'Here it is.'

They waited.

'Angelica,' she began.

Tony saw a tall, slim woman with huge bright wings fanning out above her, but the Toad Lady was hurrying on.

'Bearberry, Black Willow.'

It was a poem. Tony wished he could join in, wished it had a chorus they could stand up and sing. Ann poked the packets with her finger.

'Bladderwrack, Blue Flag.

Bogbean, Boneset, Burdock.

Cayenne, Celery Seed, Couchgrass,

Dandelion, Devil's Claw,

Guaiacum, Ginger,

Juniper

Mountain grape, Mustard,

Nettles,

Poke Root, Prickly Ash,

Ragwort,

Sarsaparilla,

White Poplar, White Yam,

Wintergreen, Wormwood,

Yarrow, Yellow Dock.'

She looked up. Ann was absorbed in the herbs, but Tony was transfixed, drunk with the wild names.

She laughed. He blushed.

'I'm sorry,' she said. 'Was it a bit of a shock? Haven't got all of these here, of course.'

'It's lovely,' he said. 'The sound of all those things.'

Miss Tasker peered over the top of her spectacles at him.

'What a strange boy you are,' she said. 'And don't you go red and angry on me again,' she warned. 'I mean it as a compliment.'

Tony did go redder, but not angry.

'Shall I read it again?'

'Yes, please.'

The Toad Lady freed Ann's fingers from the herbs, moved her closer to herself and made her follow the words with her finger as she read them out to Tony. This time she did not race through them like a shopping list, but chanted them like an incantation. She sang out Angelica and Yarrow; she growled through Bladderwrack, Bogbean, Boneset; she stiffened her fingers and raked the air as she snarled Devil's Claw; she hissed Wormwood with a poisonous menace. All the names came alive under her charm. In the silence that followed Tony breathed in the scents and aromas he imagined from all the names.

'Well then,' Miss Tasker broke in. 'Let's find something for your mother.'

'Not Devil's Claw,' Tony said quickly.

'No, not Devil's Claw. I haven't got that. But it's a jolly good herb. I'd give it to her if I had it,' she threatened him. 'But I think Celery Seed's the best thing I've got.'

Tony was happier with that.

'Here we are,' she triumphed, pulling a thick envelope from the pile. 'Crush a teaspoonful of seeds, pour boiling water on them, let it stand for a couple of minutes and drink it like tea. All right?'

'Thank you.'

'And what do you think this is?' she demanded,

tossing the forked root at him.

'Old parsnip,' said Tony.

'Turnip,' said Ann.

'Rarer than that. Try again?'

They shook their heads.

'What if I told you,' she leaned forward conspiratorially, 'that it was thought that anyone who pulled this up would die?'

'How would you get it, then?' argued Ann.

'Trained dogs to sniff them out and dig them up,' the Toad Lady told her gleefully.

'What's it called?' asked Tony.

But the Toad Lady was enjoying her game. 'And they say,' she added, 'that it screamed when it was pulled out of the earth.'

'Screamed?' asked Tony.

She nodded. 'It liked being where it was, and it screamed when you disturbed it and uprooted it.'

Tony and Ann looked doubtfully at each other, then at her. She was waiting for something, for a question. Tony really wanted to get it right, to show her how much he was learning. Ann waited. He remembered the hunt for the toad flax.

'Where does it grow?' he asked, delighted by the show of pleasure on Miss Tasker's face, to see that he had asked the right question.

'Beneath the gallows,' she hissed. 'Where they've hanged a man.'

Tony wished he hadn't asked.

'That's why it's shaped like a man,' she added.

'I don't believe any of it,' Ann said.

'Quite right,' agreed Miss Tasker. 'But those are the stories. And this,' she tossed the root to Tony, 'is Mandrake. Here. You can have this one.'

Tony fumbled the catch but he held it.

The forked root could easily pass for legs, but it needed a lot of imagination to see a man in the upper part. It looked just like a man to Tony.

'Go on. Clear out,' said the Toad Lady suddenly. 'I've got the washing up to do.'

'We'll help,' offered Tony, happy to be rewarded with her refusal.

'No. I want you all out of the way. I've got other things to do. Clear off.' Her tone was so cheerfully brutal that Tony knew she just wanted them to enjoy the rest of the afternoon.

'Thank you for lunch,' he remembered to say. 'And for the herbs.'

'Clear off,' she raised her voice. 'Before I do make you do the washing up.

He grinned and darted out with Ann.

The sun hammered down heavily on the fields and lanes. They headed down the road until they came to a stile. Tony lifted his bike over and pushed it along a dirt track into the pattern of fields. In springtime the track was often too muddy to cycle along, poached in the gateways in the deep holes made by cows' feet, or churned up by horses hooves along its length. Now, baked hard in the sun, it was bumpy but not difficult to ride along.

Tony got to the haystack first and threw himself on to it. It was small and scruffy, bales of hay falling higgledy-piggledy around. The boys had moved them about and tunnelled through them. They piled them in slopes and slid down, destroying the binding and letting them split open. Soon, this one would disappear, taken by the farmer into his cattle sheds and stables for winter feed. It was last year's grass, old and losing its flavour. The second new hay of the year was already lying cut in the fields, drying in the sun. It would be gathered, baled up and brought over to make a new stack, sharp-edged, neat and firm. The new hay sent up sweet fragrances of grass and field flowers. The old was musty and stuffy. The winter cold and rain had washed and frozen away its beauty. Ann scrambled up happily pulling handfuls of hay loose as she went. A nimbus of dust rose around her.

Tony lay back, shaded by the angle of a crazily-tottering bale, and stared up at the deep blue of the sky. The day was unbearably hot. In his scratchy nest Tony was sheltered from the sun. After he had been still for several minutes there were little scufflings below him and he knew that the rats had forgotten him and were coming out to scavenge.

Ann called down to him. 'You like her, don't you?'

Tony screwed his head round and looked up at her, so that she could see his lips. 'Yes. But I can't work her out.'

136

'What do you mean?'

'Sometimes she's so kind, so gentle. Then others she's just as sharp as any grown-up.'

'Just as what?'

'Sharp,' Tony mouthed clearly.

'Oh, that.'

'Why?'

'I don't know. Does it matter?'

Tony's neck was hurting. 'Why don't you come down if you want to talk?'

'All right.' Ann threw herself down the side of the hay with a reckless abandon that frightened Tony and he slithered out of the way. For a moment he thought that she was more like Steve and George than he was, more like a boy than a girl. But he was a boy. Perhaps there was more to it than that.

'She's kind to me, anyway,' Ann explained.

Tony was listening closely to her voice now. Since he'd learned about her deafness he was curious to notice what difference it made. There was the deepness that he had always heard, but there was a small slurring of some sounds as well. It was a bit like hearing someone who was drunk. He decided he would try to immitate it when he was on his own; not to make fun, just to see what it felt like.

'I'm going into hospital,' said Ann. 'When I go home.'

'Home?' asked Tony. Ann lived with the Toad Lady. That was her home.

'Yes. You remember. I'm only staying here for the summer.'

'Oh, yes.' Tony remembered sadly.

'Summer's nearly over,' said Ann. 'So, I'm going home.' She pulled a face.

'Don't you want to?'

'I suppose.'

'I've never been away from home,' said Tony. 'I'd want to go back.'

'Yes,' agreed Ann. 'I want to be home. But I love it here. And I love Miss Tasker.'

It seemed astonishing to Tony that anyone could talk like that about love without blushing, but Ann didn't seem to mind. And almost more astonishing that Ann could love the Toad Lady.

'It won't hurt,' said Ann.

'What?'

'The operation. I told you. They're going to do something to my ears. Put something in them I think.'

'Don't you know?' asked Tony.

'They haven't told me all about it yet. They'll do that when I get back. Anyway, it means I might be able to hear some things again.'

'That's good,' said Tony. 'Really good.'

'Not everything. Not the way you can. But something. I want that a lot, I think. I've loved being here. The smell of everything – fields and flowers and herbs, even the muck from the animals. And the colours are better here. And I love the sun and the hot hay. But I do want to hear things if I can. I don't mind that I can't,' she said, with a defiant look at Tony, that made him so uncomfortable that he forgot to be puzzled at how quickly she had said two completely opposite things. 'But if I can I want to. I don't mind having an operation if I can hear some of the things that you can hear.'

'No,' agreed Tony. 'I mean, yes.'

Tony took a deep breath, hardly believing that he could say what he was going to say. 'Well,' he began. 'I'll miss you. When are you going home?'

Ann was looking away and she didn't see him ask her. She scrambled about in her skirt pocket and brought out a sort of empty leather purse. 'She told me to show you this.'

'Me?' Tony was pleased, he thought.

'Yes. She said you were interested in toads.' Ann did not add that there had been a strange look in Miss Tasker's eye when she said it and that she laughed when she gave Ann the little leather bundle. The Toad Lady had a very naughty sense of humour.

Tony took the purse from Ann. He turned it over in his hands, examining it. There wasn't a catch or a zip, but there was certainly a hole to put things in, and it was decorated with bumps and coloured patterns. Near to the hole were two indentations, like eyes. He held it to his face and then suddenly dropped it. Ann laughed.

'You've worked it out then?' she said, and

picked it up and waggled it. It was like a trick picture; once you knew the trick it was easy but it wasn't obvious at first. The little leather bundle was a hollowed-out dried toad.

'Did she do that?' he asked.

'No. It was like that when she found it. Do you want to know what happened?'

Tony did.

Ann spoke in sing-song voice when she told him about it. She had learned her lesson from Miss Tasker and was trying not to forget any of it.

Tony's eyes widened while she spoke.

'There's an insect,' she said, 'called the green-bottle fly.'

'Ten green bottles,' laughed Tony, but Ann was looking away from him and she did not hear. He was glad immediately because it seemed a foolish interruption.

'This fly,' she went on, 'lays its eggs on the toad's skin, and then, when they hatch out the little grubs crawl into its eyes.'

'Ugh,' said Tony. Ann caught the grimace on his face and she nodded.

'It's horrible, isn't it? Well, it gets worse. After that they swim into the bit where tears come out and down into the nose. Then they grow bigger and bigger and eat the toad up from inside.'

'No,' Tony objected.

Ann saw his lips move and she nodded.

'Yes. Until all that's left is . . .' and she held

140

up the dried pouch that Tony had dropped.

'That's horrible,' said Tony.

'Yes,' she agreed. 'I used to think I was like that, like a toad that was being eaten up from the inside.'

'What?'

'Because of the meningitis. I thought I'd been eaten by things and that there was less of me than there should be. Miss Tasker told me the story to show me I was wrong. She told me so that I could see what it was really like to be eaten up by something.'

Tony didn't answer. He pulled lengths of hay away from their bales, pushed them up to his nose and drew in deep draughts of their scent.

'Funny,' he said after a long time. 'When you smell grass being cut it's lovely, clean and fresh and full of juice. But then, later, when it's been in the haystack . . .' Ann was looking at his lips very carefully as he spoke. 'It's still a good smell, but it's different, really different.'

Ann pulled out a handful of hay and smelled. While her head was bent away from him Tony deliberately spoke to her so that she couldn't hear.

'I didn't mean to say that,' he said to her closed ears, 'that about the hay. What I meant to say, what I wanted to say was that there are lots of other things that can eat you up from the inside. There are . . .'

'Tony. Tony.'

He sprang up and lost his footing. The hay underneath him gave way and he half-tumbled, half-slid down on to the field.

'Over here, Tony,' yelled Steve.

Ann slid down after him and they stood together as Steve and George ran across the field, dodging their path between thistles and cow pats. Tony clenched his fists and moved away from Ann so that he was not too close to her.

'We're wanted,' Steve announced.

'Where?'

'The vicar's. Old Nellie Hodgson is with him.'

'It's the book,' said George.

'Yes,' said Steve. 'I said we'd fetch you.'

'Right,' mumbled Tony. 'Right, then. We'll go.'

'You go,' said Steve. Doesn't concern us.'

'What is it?' asked Ann.

'Nothing,' said Tony. 'It's nothing.'

Steve grinned unpleasantly at them. Tony rounded on him.

'You were there,' he said. 'You were both there. You made me do it.'

Steve raised his eyebrows. 'Me?' he said in horror. 'Do that? I don't know anything about it. Not my writing.'

Tony ran off without a word. Ann climbed back in the hay stack and searched for the dry, empty skin of the toad. When she had found it and put it back in her pocket Steve had gone.

13

Uprooted

Nobody in the vicar's study looked very comfortable. Mrs Hodgson was struggling to stop a smile of triumph breaking through her anger. Tony's mum looked at him when he walked in with the vicar and then looked away quickly. She fidgeted with her handbag. The vicar himself had smiled when he opened the front door to Tony, but then he had been very serious when he sat down.

'Er, perhaps you'd like to sit on the sofa next to your mum?' he asked Tony.

'He can stand,' snapped Mrs Hodgson.

Tony's mum started to say something, but the Vicar interrupted.

'I'd be more comfortable if you'd sit next to your mum, Tony,' he said. So Tony sat. The temptation to smile faded from Mrs Hodgson and she set her mouth in a hard line.

'This is quite difficult to talk about,' apologized the vicar. He lifted the edge of the cover of the visitors' book.

'I did it,' said Tony.

'That's it,' said Mrs Hodgson. I told you it was his writing. I'd know it anywhere. I taught him how.'

'Then it's a pity you didn't teach him better what to write and where,' said Tony's mum sharply.

Tony's mouth fell open in astonishment. He had never heard grown-ups argue about him before, not taking sides. He smiled at his mum in gratitude.

'And you've nothing to smile about, my lad,' she warned him. 'I'll deal with you later, on my own.'

Tony's smile faded and he kicked the back of his heels against the sofa. He should have known they would all be against him in the end.

'Who put you up to it?' his mother demanded.

Tony didn't answer.

'Come on, my lad. Who was it?'

'No one.'

'He's always in and out of that church,' said Mrs Hodgson. 'On his own and with the others.'

'He wouldn't do that unless he was put up to it. I know that.'

'Well, Tony? asked the vicar.

'On my own,' said Tony.

'Well, I think that looks after things,' said the vicar, standing up. 'Perhaps you and your mother will stay on for a moment, Tony. To sort this out. Thank you Mrs Hodgson.' He stood over her chair and offered her his hand. 'Thank you for bringing this matter to my attention.'

Mrs Hodgson half stood, then sat down again.

'But what will we do about him?'

'I think that is for me to decide,' he smiled. 'Thank you.' He almost lifted Mrs Hodgson out of her chair but with such great politeness that she could not refuse.

'I must . . .' she protested.

'I think Tony has left the school now,' he said.

'Yes.'

'And the visitor's book is the property of the church. So I must decide what punishment or repayment to ask from Tony.'

Mrs Hodgson found herself at the vicarage doorstep.

'Thank you. Thank you,' he smiled as the door closed.

The sound of Tony's mum's voice cut through the closed door of the study, punctuated from time to time by short protests from Tony. These protests were hacked away as she laid into him. The vicar retreated into his kitchen and came back five minutes later. His hands were full and he had to kick the door several times with his foot before Tony let him in.

'Coffee,' he said to Tony's mum.

'Oh, no. Really. We'd best be going once you've decided what to do with Tony.'

'I've made it now,' he argued. 'And orange

juice for Tony. And biscuits,' he added, passing the plate round.

Again, it was impossible to refuse him, so Tony's mum accepted her cup.

'Not that you should be giving him biscuits after what he's done to you,' she complained.

'What will you do to me?' Tony asked before he put the glass to his lips.

'I've done it,' the vicar replied.

Tony's mum pursed her lips.

'You should have asked me first,' she said. Then she jumped. 'Not the police?' she said in alarm. 'You haven't rung the police. Not just for a book.' Her surprise turned to anger. 'It was only a book,' she insisted. 'And only one page at that. He's not a bad lad, our Tony. He's led, but he's not bad.'

The vicar held up a hand to interrupt her. 'Please,' he said. 'Please. I'm glad you say that. That it was only one page of one book. And that he's not a bad lad. I know that.'

'So why?' asked Tony.

'The police?' he smiled. 'I never said anything about the police.'

Tony's mum shifted uncomfortably.

'I think,' the vicar concluded. 'That as he did actually write in the book, no matter who encouraged him to,' he pointed a finger at Tony to silence his protests. 'No matter who encouraged him to,' he continued. ' then he must be punished. And I decided that five minutes in here with his mother telling him what a stupid thing it was to do was quite enough. Don't you?' he asked them both. When there was no answer he said. 'Well, then. Let that be an end to it.'

Tony breathed a sigh of relief, even though he knew that there would be more later when he got home.

'Will you, please?' the vicar asked Tony's mum.

'He shouldn't have . . .' she began.

'Yes, I know. And he knows now. Please. Can this be an end of it?'

Tony was amazed to see that his mother's eyes filled with tears as she nodded. He was even more surprised when she gripped his hand very hard. It upset him and he felt his own eyes grow damp. This was awful. He glared at the vicar for upsetting them all like that.

'Sorry, Tony,' he apologized. 'Sometimes it's more difficult to be treated gently.'

Tony nodded. He drew the packet of seeds out of his pocket.

'These are for your, you know – your back,' he said.

Tony's mother turned her face away from him for a moment before she could look at him with a smile. George was waiting outside with Ann when Tony left the vicarage. Steve was nowhere to be seen.

'I've come to tell him,' said George, ignoring the vicar.

'Doesn't matter,' said Tony. 'He knew anyway.'

'You'll stay a minute, won't you?' the vicar encouraged Tony's mum. She nodded. 'Where's Steve?' he asked George.

'It was nothing to do with Steve,' George protested. 'I told Tony to.'

'Oh, dear,' said the vicar, and he closed the door on the three children.

'Come on,' said Ann.

'Where?' asked George.

'Never mind,' said Tony. 'Come on.'

They crossed the fields and cut over the public footpath that took them safely past the railway line. The haystack sagged and crumbled.

'If we climb right to the top you can see my new school,' said Tony.

They boosted each other up the slipping bales.

'Just there,' Tony pointed. The stack rocked and subsided beneath them. Ann nearly fell and she clutched George for security. The great panes of glass gleamed dully at them from beneath the flat roof of the school. The old buildings had gone long before they stopped making people take exams to go there.

'Not long now,' said George.

Tony looked at the lowering sun reflecting at them from the giant windows. He took out the

149

mandrake root and held it between him and the school, then he opened his mouth wide and let out a huge, deep scream.

'What?' demanded George.

'No,' agreed Tony. 'Not long now.'

They tobogganed down the hay and rolled to the bottom.

'Come on,' Ann repeated.

Large spots of rain disturbed the surface of the brook. The children were kept dry by the overhang of the trees and the broad leaves. The drops pattered down, spreading and sinking into the dry earth. A delicious, secret scent broke out from the land as the rain seeped through. It was as hot as ever even though the blue sky had broken up.

'No,' said George, at last, when the Toad Lady's cottage came into view. 'I don't want to.'

'She's all right,' Tony reassured him. 'She's nice.'

'No,' said George. He turned to go.

'Don't be frightened,' Tony mocked him.

George turned back. He pointed to Ann's face. 'Look.'

Ann, who had forgotten the marks of the cuts put surprised fingers to her cheek.

'Look,' said George. 'I'm sorry. About that, I mean.'

'I don't mind,' said Ann. 'Come on.'

'No,' said George. 'She knows. I'm not coming.'

'Please,' said Tony. 'I want you to meet her.'

George pushed his way through the long grass and out of sight.

The kitchen was dry and bright after the wet dullness outside, beautiful with the scent of the many bunches of flowers and herbs.

'Ann leaves tomorrow,' said the Toad Lady.

'Oh.'

Ann watched Tony's mouth.

'She's going to miss the toads,' Miss Tasker went on.

There was a very long pause before Miss Tasker said.

'You see, Ann lives in a town and doesn't see many animals or wild flowers. That's why she's enjoyed them so much here. She didn't know anything about them before.

'Neither did I,' admitted Tony. 'Not about toads. Nor about the names of all those flowers. Not till you told me.'

Miss Tasker ignored this.

'I could write to her,' he offered.

'Yes,' Miss Tasker agreed. 'Yes, you could. Would you like that, Ann?'

Ann was already smiling before Miss Tasker asked her.

'And perhaps you'd like to come here sometimes and have tea with me?' Miss Tasker suggested. 'I'd like some help pressing new herbs in my book. That is,' she paused and looked slyly at Ann.

'If you wouldn't mind being on your own with the Toad Lady.'

Ann looked very cross. Tony blushed. Then they all saw each other's faces and began to laugh.

'No,' said Tony. 'I wouldn't mind. I'd like that a lot.'

'And I'll be coming back for my next holiday,' said Ann.

'Well. That's settled, then,' said the Toad Lady.

RT, MARGARET AND THE RATS OF NIMH
Jane Leslie Conly

When Margaret and her brother RT get lost in the forests surrounding Thorn Valley, help comes from an unexpected quarter when the super-rats of NIMH come to their rescue. Margaret and RT must return home before winter sets in, but the incredible events of their summer in the valley become the biggest secret they have ever had to keep.

The third thrilling story in this classic trilogy about the rats of NIMH.

ONLY MIRANDA
Tessa Krailing

A new town, a tiny flat over the Chinese takeaway, a new school mid-term and a place next to Chrissie Simpson, the most unpopular girl in the class. Things aren't looking great for Miranda. But her father has gone to prison and this at least is a chance of a new life for her and her mother. Miranda bounces back in true style: she befriends poor Chrissie and when the dinner money is stolen and Chrissie is suspected, Miranda is determined to prove her innocence.

TWIN AND SUPER TWIN
Gillian Cross

Ben, David and Mitch had only meant to start the Wellington Street Gang's bonfire, not blow up all their fireworks as well. But even worse is what happens to David's arm in the process. Until, that is, they realize that this extraordinary event could be very useful in their battles with the Wellington Street Gang.

WOLF

Gillian Cross

Cassy has never understood the connection between the secret midnight visitor to her nan's flat and her sudden trips to
stay with her mother. But this time it seems different. She
finds her mother living in a squat with her boyfriend Lyall
and his son Robert. Lyall has devised a theatrical event for
children on wolves, and Cassy is soon deeply involved in
presenting it. Perhaps too involved – for she begins to sense a
very real and terrifying wolf stalking her.

THE OUTSIDE CHILD

Nina Bawden

Imagine suddenly discovering you have a step-brother and
-sister no one has ever told you about! It's the most exciting
thing that's ever happened to Jane, and she can't wait to
meet them. Perhaps at last she will become part of a 'proper'
family, instead of for ever being the outside child. So begins
a long search for her brother and sister, but when she finally
does track them down, Jane finds there are still more sur-
prises in store!

THE FOX OF SKELLAND

Rachel Dixon

Samantha's never liked the old custom of Foxing Day – the
fox costume especially gives her the creeps. So when Jason
and Rib, children of the new publications at The Fox and
Lady, find the costume and Jason wears it to the fancy-dress
disco, she's sure something awful will happen.

Then Sam's old friend Joseph sees the ghost of the Lady and
her fox. Has she really come back to exact vengeance on the
village? Or has her appearance got something to do with the
spate of burglaries in the area?

STORMSEARCH
Robert Westall

It is Tim who finds the model ship buried in the sand and, with growing excitement, he, his sister Tracey and their eccentric Uncle Geoff realize the significance of their discovery. For the model ship yields up a long-forgotten secret and a story of danger and romance.

THE WATER HORSE
Dick King-Smith

Last night's storm has washed up a strange object like a giant mermaid's purse, which Kirstie takes home and puts in the bath. The next day it has hatched into a tiny greeny-grey creature, with a horse's head, a warty skin, four flippers and a crocodile's tail. The adorable baby sea monster soon becomes the family pet – but the trouble is, he just doesn't stop growing!

WILL THE REAL GERTRUDE HOLLINGS PLEASE STAND UP?
Sheila Greenwald

Gertrude is in a bad way. She's a bit slow at school but everyone thinks she's dumb and her teachers call her 'Learning Disabled' behind her back. As if this isn't enough, her parents go off on a business trip leaving her with her aunt and uncle and her obnoxious cousin, Albert – a 'superachiever'. Gertrude is determined to win Perfect Prize-Winning Albert's respect by whatever means it takes ...